"He was in S0-ADG-741

The cushion beside her sank and the balance shifted as George sat down. "I believe you." He pulled both her hands between his and gently rubbed them.

His simple statement of faith in her sanity swept out the cobwebs of self-doubt and touched her bruised heart.

Curling her legs beneath her, Elise pushed herself up, looping her arms about George's neck, knocking him into the back of the couch. "Thank you."

He folded his arms around her, flattening one hand against her spine to anchor her to his body. He pushed aside the jacket's collar and threaded his fingers into the short hair at her nape to massage the tension in her neck.

"You're okay. You're safe now. No one's going to hurt you."

KCPD PROTECTOR

USA TODAY Bestselling Author
JULIE MILLER

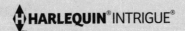

HARLEQUIN® INTRIGUE®

Recycling programs
for this product may
not exist in your area.

To Pam Jones-Hamblin and Jenny Simons—
two sisters who compete to see who can
read my books first. Too much fun!
And what a lovely compliment.

I'm happy to be a part of the competition.

ISBN-13: 978-0-373-74830-3

KCPD PROTECTOR

Copyright © 2014 by Julie Miller

Printed in U.S.A.

ABOUT THE AUTHOR

USA TODAY bestselling author Julie Miller attributes her passion for writing romance to all those books she read growing up. When shyness and asthma kept her from becoming the action-adventure heroine she longed to be, Julie created stories in her head to keep herself entertained. Encouragement from her family to write down the feelings and ideas she couldn't express became a love for the written word. She gets continued support from her fellow members of the Prairieland Romance Writers, where this teacher serves as the resident "grammar goddess." Inspired by the likes of Agatha Christie and Encyclopedia Brown, Julie believes the only thing better than a good mystery is a good romance.

Born and raised in Missouri, this award-winning author now lives in Nebraska with her husband, son and an assortment of spoiled pets. To contact Julie or to learn more about her books, write to P.O. Box 5162, Grand Island, NE 68802-5162 or check out her website and monthly newsletter at www.juliemiller.org.

Books by Julie Miller

HARLEQUIN INTRIGUE

CAST OF CHARACTERS

George Madigan—Deputy Commissioner of the KCPD. He's an old-school, by-the-book man's man with a badge. The one rule he's tempted to break? Getting personal with the leggy brunette who runs his office like clockwork. But when a campaign of psychological terror threatens his assistant, this career cop puts his life on the line to protect the city...and the woman he's falling for.

Elise Brown—Three strikes and you're out in the relationship department. With her humiliating track record with men, Elise has given up on love and devoted herself to her work in the deputy commissioner's office. But when a dangerous stalker turns her well-ordered life upside down, she relies on one man she trusts, the one man she knows she can never have—her boss.

James Westbrook—Elise almost married him back in college. But career opportunities took them in different directions. Does he want her back in his life?

Courtney Reiter—George's needy ex-wife can't seem to let him go.

Denton Hale—A police officer worried about his job. And maybe he should be.

Quinn Gallagher—Elise's former boss. She once thought he'd be the love of her life. Now she's lucky this business tycoon is still a friend.

Alexsandr Titov—The brother of a slain mob boss. Why is he in Kansas City? And how much does he know about Elise's relationship with his late brother?

Shane Wilkins—A young, ambitious police officer George mentors. He takes his job guarding the command floor of KCPD headquarters very seriously.

Nick & Annie Fensom—George's nephew and niece-in-law—a KCPD detective and a CSI who understand the meaning of family helping family.

Spike—The best guard dog ever...if not necessarily the most intimidating.

Mother Nature—Her summer heat wave and violent storms have the entire city on edge.

Chapter One

"Elise? I need—"

"Right here." As soon as the lacquered black door between their offices opened, Elise Brown was on her feet, carrying the file from the corner of her desk over to her boss, KCPD Deputy Commissioner George Madigan. "Crime rate statistics for the downtown area over the past three years. I also checked the Farmers' Almanac for the last time Kansas City had record temperatures like this and forwarded stats on the dramatic rise in reported crime incidents for that summer to your laptop. I pulled up similar stats on the increased number of 9-1-1 calls during power outages."

"And my dinner—?"

"Done. I called the restaurant and moved your reservation this evening back to eight o'clock. Your appointment will meet you there."

George's firm mouth cocked into a wry grin, deepening the lines beside his steel-gray eyes as he opened the folder. "You might at least let me finish asking my questions before you hand over the answers."

George Madigan didn't ask—he gave orders—but Elise didn't mind. She tipped her face up to his and smiled. "Just being indispensable."

"That you are. I swear you could do this job without me. But I wouldn't manage the other way around. Thanks." He dropped his gaze to the information he held, thumbing through the pages, already engrossed in his work.

Elise smiled at the crown of his dark brown hair. It was short and thick and peppered with shots of silver that only added to the mature air of masculinity that oozed from every pore. Not that she cared one whit about how the man looked or what he oozed. All she cared about was this job and the way George valued her as a trusted associate.

There were no miscommunications when her boss spoke. No flirty double entendres she had to evaluate and dodge. No favors or blackmail or anything that could leave her feeling like a fool for not clearly understanding what was being asked of her.

She appreciated the mutual respect in their working relationship, and had no intention of muddying the waters by wishing there might be a little more charm to his authoritative demeanor or wondering how a full-blown smile or belly laugh might soften the life experience sculpted into his angular features.

The deputy commissioner and KCPD had taken a chance on her when her confidence had been so close to rock bottom that she wasn't sure she even deserved a job in the corporate world again. Working as an executive assistant for one of the top administrators in the department, she was rebuilding the self-assurance that had been shredded at her last full-time position. Fixing her bruised heart and shattered trust in men were projects for another day. For her, the job was enough. It was everything. It had to be.

"This is good stuff," George praised. "These numbers should help make my case for allocating more funds."

"You hired me to be knowledgeable, efficient and to anticipate your needs."

To make her point, she flipped the page to point out the totals he was searching for and nodded toward the office behind him where five people sat around a cherrywood conference table, engaged in a heated discussion studded with phrases like "We're already short staffed," "Not my responsibility," "How much?"

and "Would you go there without a cop around for miles?"

Elise didn't even need to drop her voice for privacy. "Emergency budget meeting? Complaints from the union about freezing salaries instead of paying overtime? The most vocal person in the room is Councilman Johnson. Ergo, you want to be armed with the information showing a direct correlation between hot weather and a higher crime rate, and how putting extra uniformed officers on the street during peak power demands will counteract that danger."

A dark eyebrow arched as he looked up from the file. "Ergo?"

Elise met his gaze and shrugged. "So you can shut up Mr. Johnson."

That earned a chuckle from deep in his throat. Okay. So the man did possess a little charm. "You're onto me. Did anyone ever tell you that you'd make a good detective?"

Elise looked beyond the wide shoulders of his blue dress shirt to see the medals and commendations framed on the wall behind his desk. Her boss's day might be filled with administrative duties now, but there was no doubt who the real detective was here. "I function much better behind the scenes than I do on the front line, sir."

His square jaw tightened momentarily. But before he snapped the folder shut and gave voice to whatever thought had crossed his features, a light knock on Elise's office door diverted her attention across the reception area.

"Hello?"

"Excuse me, sir." Elise crossed the taupe carpet to meet the deliveryman hidden behind the extravagant bouquet of yellow roses at the hallway door. "Yes?"

"Is this the deputy commissioner's office?" a winded voice asked.

"It is."

"Finally. Do you know how far I had to carry these things?" When the twentysomething man poked his head around the tall glass vase, his ruddy cheeks and forehead were dotted with perspiration. She also noted that he was wearing a visitor's badge around the sweat-stained neck of his brown uniform. Good. That meant he'd been cleared at both the ground floor and the security desk at the eighth floor elevators, and she didn't need to screen him as any kind of threat to the higher-ups at KCPD.

"Has it topped a hundred degrees out there yet?" Elise asked, reaching for the electronic signature pad he pushed toward her. Since a heat wave was bearing down on Kansas City for its third straight week, it was a topic of conversation friends and strangers alike could share. She hoped her friendly smile might improve the man's mood.

But she got little more than a weary grunt in return. "I just need you to sign for these, ma'am."

Understanding how a heat index of one hundred and ten and humidity that was nearly as high could make tempers and frustrations flare, Elise quickly wrote her name. "Could I get you something cold to drink? Some ice water?"

The man's grim expression relaxed as he traded the vase for the keypad. "I've got a cooler in my van in the parking garage across the street. But thanks."

"Looks like Commissioner Madigan has a special admirer." Elise hefted the over-the-top bouquet into her arms. Had George won some award he hadn't mentioned? Been seeing someone during the few hours he wasn't in the office?

"They're for you, ma'am." The deliveryman glanced down at his keypad screen. "You're Elise Brown, right?"

Surprise warred with confusion inside her at the unexpected gift. "For me?"

"Yes, ma'am. Enjoy. And stay cool." The man was all smiles as he walked away.

Elise touched her nose to one velvety blossom, cautiously inhaling its cloying, perfumey scent as she counted. Eleven, twelve...twenty-three yellow roses, complete with golden ribbons, baby's breath and a cut-glass vase—for her?

The flowers grew unbearably heavy. *Twenty-three roses. One for every day we've been together.*

"Easy." Suddenly, a strong hand cupped beneath hers, taking the weight of the glass. "We don't want a flood on the carpet."

A flash of blue danced into Elise's peripheral vision a split second before her boss's crisp voice startled her from her momentary paralysis. She backed away a step and hugged her arms securely around the vase. "I've got them." She turned and carried them to the corner of her desk. "Thanks."

The flowers might be a different color, but the similarity...twenty-three? Elise breathed in deeply, clearing the troubling thought from her mind. It wasn't possible. The florist had simply miscounted. Or the deliveryman had stolen one for his girlfriend. This was just a coincidence and she'd overreacted. That part of her past was over and done with.

Dead men didn't send flowers.

But who would?

Shuffling through the stems and greenery, Elise searched for a card that wasn't there. She pulled the empty plastic clamp from the vase that should have held the sender's name or a message for her, and hurried out into the hallway. "Wait a minute," she called after the deliveryman. "Who are these from? There's no card…."

But he'd already disappeared around the corner by the elevators and security desk. She could either kick off her heels and run after him, or solve the mystery on her own. And since Nikolai was dead… With another steadying breath, Elise had made her decision. *Ease up on the paranoia. There's a rational explanation. Figure it out.*

But when she turned around, she froze, her path blocked by George Madigan filling the doorway. His sturdy forearms were exposed by his rolled-up sleeves, and their tanned strength formed an impenetrable barrier folded across the front of his chest. "Did I miss your birthday?"

Although he wore no gun, his badge was

right there, clipped to his belt, its polished blue enamel and extra brass chevrons indicating he had the right to stop her and ask any questions he wanted in this office. Elise tipped her face up to his narrowed gray eyes. Was that suspicion she saw there? Curiosity? Concern?

She knew that George Madigan on a mission could be an intimidating thing. His devotion to the department, his single-minded determination to solve problems, made him a force to be reckoned with in city and departmental politics. But the idea of him turning that perceptive intelligence and laser beam focus on her was as unnerving as it was thrilling.

And that made those little ripples of awareness stirring her blood far too dangerous.

Tempting as it might be to share her fears with her boss, Elise nixed the idea. Her problems were her own. She understood George Madigan well enough to get her job done, and that was as far as their relationship needed to go. Mixing work and personal was definitely a bad idea.

"Elise?"

Oh, snap. How long had she been staring at the loose knot of his tie?

Despite the air-conditioning that cooled the building's temperature to a tolerable level, Elise suddenly felt hot. She brushed aside a short dark wave of hair that clung to her damp skin and tucked it behind her ear before scooting around the file he fisted in one hand. "My birthday's not until September."

Two months away. Elise set the card holder beside the vase and sorted through the ribbons and greenery again. She found one broken stem being held upright by sprigs of baby's breath and the oversize bow, but still no card.

A queasy sense of unease turned in her stomach. Nikolai had sent her twenty-three red roses after he'd gone back to Russia. A thank-you, apology and *do svidaniya* all in one. But Nikolai was dead. Murdered by her former boss Quinn Gallagher's father-in-law when Nikolai had dared to threaten Quinn's daughter.

"I know it's not Administrative Professionals' Week. I marked that on my calendar." George followed her to the desk and reached out to finger one of the blooms. "These are unexpected."

It wasn't a question.

"Yes," she conceded, wishing she could mask her emotions as well as her boss could. "They're definitely a surprise."

The only men in her life were her father and her poodle mix, Spike, and neither one was the flower-sending type. Her mother was the one to remember special events, but nothing was happening in Elise's life today, or even this week. She hadn't completed the renovations on the Victorian home she was restoring, so any celebration of that was premature. Successfully housebreaking the dog hardly merited all these flowers. And the last man she'd gone out with certainly had no reason to send such a gift. Although they'd once shared a college romance, she'd made it clear to James this past weekend that she was only interested in friendship now that he was back in town after spending several years working abroad.

After her disastrous track record of unrequited love and getting involved with the wrong men, she wasn't interested in any kind of relationship.

Elise startled at the warm hand on her arm and looked up into George's eyes. "What's wrong?"

She jumped again when the telephone rang. Shaking off his touch and any further speculation about the roses, she leaned across her desk and picked up the receiver. "Deputy Commissioner Madigan's office. This is Elise speaking."

There was a long pause on the line, and then she heard, "Did you get them?"

The hushed, breathy voice was barely audible.

"Excuse me?"

"I got them special. Just for you."

Suddenly feeling too shaky to stand, Elise sank onto the edge of the cherrywood desk and turned her head toward the mysterious bouquet. "Who is this?"

The phone was pried from her grip by a stronger hand. "This is Deputy Commissioner Madigan of KCPD. Who—?"

The click of the call disconnecting was loud enough for Elise to hear. When she jerked her head back toward the sound, her gaze was filled with George's paisley tie and broad chest. That chest came even closer, almost folded around her, as he reached behind her to hang up the phone.

Elise pushed to her feet, curling her toes inside her pumps to steady herself, when she realized she'd nearly turned her nose into the inviting haven of the older man's crisp shirt and body heat.

But George didn't move. He stood there, feet planted like tree trunks to the floor, watching her reaction. "What's going on?"

Rubbing at the goose bumps revealed by her sleeveless dress, Elise shrugged off her confusion about the flowers as well as that sudden and inexplicable urge to take shelter against her boss's chest. "I have no idea."

George tossed the file onto her desk and quickly inspected the bouquet. "You don't know who these are from?" He didn't give her time to answer. "Did you recognize the caller on the phone?"

Elise shook her head. "I think it was a man's voice, but he was whispering. I could barely hear him. I would have thought it was a wrong number, but he…asked about the flowers. At least, I think that's what he meant. He didn't actually say 'flowers.'"

"I didn't catch a company logo on the deliveryman's shirt. Did you?" George was already headed for the hallway before she realized his intent. "I'll check with Shane at the front desk to see if he remembers the uniform. He should have logged him in, so we can at least get a name and who he works for. Then we can call and find out who ordered them."

Elise hurried after George, stopping him with a hand on his arm before he got out the door. "You don't have to go to all that trouble."

"Clearly, not knowing where these came from has upset you." He turned to face her. "I may spend my days balancing numbers and taking meetings, but I'm still a cop. I know when something doesn't smell right, and I remember how to track down a lead."

"But there's no crime here, Commissioner. And it's not your job to take care of me." As easy as it would be to let him find answers for her, Elise knew he had more important things to worry about than her self-conscious paranoia about mysterious romantic gestures. "If anything, I'm supposed to take care of you. I'll talk to Shane before I leave this evening." She nodded toward his office. "Besides, you're keeping the councilman and precinct chiefs waiting, and with this weather crisis, tempers are already shorter than usual. You need to return to your meeting."

"You're sure?" He glanced down at the spot where her pale fingers still clung to his tanned, muscular forearm.

Feeling her cheeks heat with embarrassment, Elise snatched her fingers away from the lingering contact and went back to her desk. "These could have been delivered to me by mistake. I'm probably just making trouble for myself by worrying about it."

It was a flimsy excuse, and George wasn't buying it. "The price of that bouquet is an awfully expensive mistake to make. Plus, the deliveryman called you by name."

This wouldn't be the first time she'd had to deal with an unwanted suitor or suffer the repercussions of a relationship mistake. She didn't have a good track record with men. But she certainly didn't want the boss she respected, and whose opinion of her she valued, to find out what a failure she was in her personal life. Whether this was someone's pathetic attempt to worm his way back into her good graces, a poorly timed coincidence or just a bad joke— she didn't want her problems to ever become a concern for George or the deputy commissioner's office.

Elise's gaze landed on the stack of pink message papers on her blotter. She circled the desk to pick them up and hand them to him. "You have three messages to handle when your meeting is done. Denton Hale has phoned twice. He wants a private meeting without the other union reps regarding possible staff cuts." Running interference between her boss and disgruntled officers and citizens was part of her job, and Elise had no problem doing it. Still, she felt a pang of sympathy, knowing how difficult a police officer's job could be without having to worry about money. "If we don't get extra funding from the city, some of the officers and support staff are going to be laid off, right?"

"It's a possibility," he answered honestly. "The city is pouring a lot of money into their infrastructure right now. I hope we can keep the personnel budget in check through attrition and simply not hire replacements for this year's retirees. I pray that's enough to avoid a strike. Hale isn't the only police officer worried about his job."

Elise nodded her understanding. "But he seems to be more worried than any of the others. He's pretty chatty on the phone. I said I'd have to discuss it with you before I scheduled it."

"Elise. What's wrong with the flowers?"

Without answering, she moved on to the next message. "Cliff Brandt from the city power district says his people have received more threats in response to the brownouts and power outages. He wants to know the result of this meeting as soon as you do. He's reluctant to let his people go out on calls unprotected, especially at night. And Mrs. Madigan said it was urgent that you return her call by five."

George was smart enough to see her diversionary tactic for what it was. But he played along, respecting her unspoken request to let the mystery of the flowers drop. "Don't stick my nose into your business, right?" Familiar lines bracketed his mouth again as he sorted through the messages. "Schedule Hale for tomorrow. Get Brandt on the phone for me in thirty minutes—it'll help me wrap up this meeting." He tucked the notes into his shirt pocket. "And Courtney's my ex-wife, not Mrs. Madigan. She gave up the right to use my name a decade ago when she said she couldn't be married to a street cop anymore. Any clue what she wants this time?"

Elise's attention shifted from the troublesome flowers to the weary sigh in George's tone. "A street cop?"

"I know. Hard to imagine, isn't it? I keep my sidearm locked in my desk and carry home budget reports instead of case files." He buttoned his collar and straightened the knot of his tie, although he didn't touch the rolled-up sleeves. "But I did my time in Vice and Narcotics once I made detective. I got into administration because I thought the desk job would make her happy. Turned out I had a knack for paper pushing and bottom lines so I stayed with it, even after she left."

Elise frowned, surprised to hear faint echoes of resignation and regret in his voice. "You still wear a badge. You're still KCPD. A lot of people in the department count on you to do your job—even if your ex-wife doesn't appreciate that."

George nodded at her show of support, even as he dismissed it. "There was more than my job wrong with our marriage." He picked up the folder he'd set down without elaborating any further. "When Court calls back, and she will—since she dropped Madigan, she must want something pretty badly—you can refer to her as Ms. Reiter."

"Yes, sir."

"Commissioner Madigan?" Henry Johnson's voice was shrill and impatient, calling from his office.

George's chest expanded with a deep breath. He checked his watch. "It's almost four o'clock. Why don't you close up shop out here. As soon as I wrap up this meeting and connect with Cliff Brandt, you can head home early. I'll lock up."

Although Elise appreciated the kind gesture, and knew she needed to go home to let Spike out into the backyard for a romp, the otherwise empty expanses of her torn-up house with its two overworked window air conditioners didn't seem particularly inviting right now. What if that phone call hadn't been a mistake and exactly twenty-three roses were meant for her? What if that ghostly voice was leaving a message on her personal answering machine or voice mail right now?

Even the unlucky coincidence of these flowers coming from James or some other old boyfriend wasn't exactly comforting. That meant her "no thanks" on a relationship hadn't registered, and that she had another long conversation, if not an outright confrontation, to look forward to this evening.

Right now, work—and the confines of her nicely appointed, if slightly humid, office—seemed more of a solace than the paint cans, phone calls or potential surprise visits that might be waiting for her at home.

"If it's all right, I'd like to stay here—I need to type up the notes for your speech at the annual officers' retirement luncheon."

George groaned. "That damned speech. If Commissioner Cartwright-Masterson wasn't expecting her first grandchild…"

Elise smiled and shooed him toward his office. "The commissioner wouldn't have asked you to take her place on the podium if she didn't trust you to represent her and the department in stellar fashion."

"That doesn't mean you need to stay late just to make me sound good at the banquet. I'll work on it. You get out of here and enjoy the AC someplace where you actually have to put on a sweater because it's so cold."

Instead of laughing at what she assumed was a joke, she offered him a half-truth. "Sounds tempting, but…I'm getting out of an unwanted date tonight with an old friend. The excuse I gave for not meeting him for dinner was that I had to work late. Do you mind?"

George arched one of his dark brows in a skeptical frown. "Maybe that unwanted date is who sent the flowers. Could be he's trying to change your mind."

"It won't."

"You should still ask him."

Elise considered the possibility. Maybe she would give James a call. But later, so he wouldn't think she'd changed her mind about his dinner invitation. "I'll check with Shane first and call the desk downstairs if he doesn't have the florist's name."

Shaking his head, George headed for his office. "Fine. I'll alibi you out. Tell Mr. Unwanted that your boss is an old curmudgeon who works your fingers until they bleed and doesn't allow you a personal life."

Elise smiled at the self-effacing comment and watched him walk away, idly noting that there was nothing old or curmudgeonly about the way his shirt hugged his powerful build. And though she knew he was more than a dozen years her senior, the lines beside his eyes and salt-and-pepper hair only added to the air of seasoned authority and masculinity he wore like a second skin. There was no mistaking George Madigan for a boyish college sweetheart or a duplicitous charmer who'd prey on her vulnerable feelings to get what he wanted from her. He was an old-school, straightforward, get-the-job-done man's man.

After an unintentional betrayal that had nearly cost her former boss at Gallagher Security Systems and his family their lives, Elise knew she was lucky to have this job. And although Quinn Gallagher claimed he didn't blame her for any of the mess that had nearly destroyed him, Elise knew she could have saved him a lot of trouble if she'd been thinking with her head instead of a broken heart. Turning in her resignation to the man she'd loved but could never have had been the right thing to do. But picking up the pieces of her life again hadn't been easy.

With that kind of personal and professional track record, Elise was grateful to have this well-paying, well-respected position doing meaningful work for the department and Kansas City. The deputy commissioner's faith in her had done more to heal her self-esteem and rebuild her trust in men than any self-help book could. That's all she should be focusing on. Noticing that George Madigan was an attractive man, noticing anything more than him as a fair leader and kind friend, could only lead to the sort of trouble she didn't need in her life.

So she ignored those little frissons of awareness that warmed her blood and sat down to work. "Thank you, sir."

He paused at the door, exhaling an audible sigh before glancing over his shoulder at her. "It's 'George' when it's just you and me talking. Okay? 'Sir' makes me feel like an old man."

Not a chance.

But before Elise could do something foolish like tell him he was a fit man in his prime, Henry Johnson shouted from his office again. "Deputy Commissioner? Today?"

With a smile that was part relief, part sympathy, Elise shooed him on his way. "You'd better not keep him waiting any longer. You want to win his support, remember?"

George paused with his hand on the doorknob, looking as if he had something more to say. Instead of speaking to Elise, though, he opened the door. "I got the file I needed, Henry. Now let's compare the costs of prevention strategies versus…"

When the door closed behind him, Elise

turned to her computer and pulled up the memos he'd sent her for distribution and started proofing and addressing them. With the discussion on the other side of George's door now muted, she worked in relative silence for several minutes.

But the bouquet was casting a shadow over her work space, drawing her attention away from her keyboard and screen. Maybe she should take the time now to walk down the hall to chat with Shane Wilkins, the floor officer. Or maybe she could spare a few minutes to call James. Or her parents. Do a little investigating on her own.

Elise rose in a huff and picked up the heavy glass vase to move the roses out of sight on the counter behind her desk. "Or maybe I should just get my work done and deal with you later. I know a nice hospital where you'll be very happy and greatly appreciated," she said to the flowers as she set them down.

With that much of a plan in mind, Elise sat down to finish the memos and save them for George's final sign-off in the morning.

Do you like my gift?

The breathy whisper seeped into her thoughts to distract her again. Who else knew that her murdered mobster lover had sent her twenty-three roses, thanking her for the unintended pillow talk regarding her former employer, making a mockery of the way she'd given her heart and body to him? Or was this just an unfortunate coincidence that she was turning into something more sinister?

Lots of people got roses every day. Red ones, pink ones, yellow ones—any color of the rainbow for any occasion or no reason at all. They didn't mean anything other than "congratulations" or "get well" or "thinking of you."

So why did it feel as though someone was looking over her shoulder now?

Elise spun her chair around and gazed at the hated gift. Then she picked it up and set the vase back on her desk.

Better to keep the things that worried her in plain sight than to let them sneak up and nearly ruin her life again.

Chapter Two

"Sorry, Spikey."

Elise laughed at the furry black bullet that shot out from beneath her spirea bushes as the first spray of water from the sprinkler hit the tiny white flowers and dark green leaves. The dog was in her lap the moment she climbed up onto the new wood deck and stretched out on the chaise lounge, demanding a tummy rub and some kind words to make up for being splashed.

"Maybe you shouldn't bury your treats out there. If you'd chew them up when I give them to you, instead of hiding them in the yard, you wouldn't risk taking an impromptu bath when I turn on the water." Elise rubbed the dog's soft, curly hair a few seconds longer, then kissed him on his head and set the miniature poodle/terrier mix on the deck beside her. "It's still too hot for a cuddle, though, you brave little toodle face. You'd better scout out the perimeter before we turn in for the night."

With a soft tap to his rump, Spike scooted down the steps and followed his nose into the grass. Elise would be happy if the warm wind shifted and misted some of the water over her bare legs, shorts and paint shirt, but not the dog. She grinned, watching Spike circle along the fence, avoiding the spray while he reclaimed his rawhide chew from beneath the bushes.

Truly relaxing for the first time today, Elise picked up the icy glass of tea on the table beside her and flicked away the condensation before taking a long drink. She touched her damp palm to the nape of her neck before leaning back to enjoy the peaceful retreat of her backyard at twilight. She figured the reprieve would last about five to ten minutes before the mosquitoes found her. But by then, she'd be heading back in to finish cleaning up from the evening's renovation work.

She took another leisurely sip, purposely letting the moisture from the glass drip onto the front of her dad's old button-down shirt and trickle beneath the placket to her hot skin. The soft, worn cotton was stained with all the colors of her remodel, including a splash of dark blue from the shutters she'd been painting for the living and dining room areas this evening.

Once, she'd dreamed of restoring a home like

this with her former boss, Quinn Gallagher, and raising a family together in the big house and spacious backyard. But Quinn, a widower who'd needed his trusted assistant to fill in as babysitter, comforter and sounding board, had fallen in love with someone else. And the need that Elise had hoped would blossom into something more had vanished in the span of a few hectic, dangerous days, leaving her reeling and alone. Easy pickings for Quinn's business associate, Nikolai Titov, who had said all the right things and made her feel wanted…and then used information she'd inadvertently shared to not only ratchet up his plot to destroy Quinn's security empire, but to murder Quinn and his daughter. Fortunately, Quinn's new wife, a rifle-toting member of KCPD's premier SWAT team, had been there to save them both.

A familiar knot of guilt and regret twisted in Elise's stomach. While she couldn't fault Quinn and his daughter for claiming happiness and moving on with their lives, there'd been no one but her parents to help her pick up the pieces of her broken dreams two years ago. And she'd been too humiliated to share everything with them. She hadn't even shared all the details with the counselor who'd evaluated her before qualifying for the job at police department headquarters. How foolish or desperate did a woman have to be to have an affair with a man, and not know until he sent her flowers from the airport as he was leaving the country that he didn't feel anything for her at all—that he'd only been using her?

Eric and Susan Brown had known something had changed in their daughter after that. They'd helped her make the down payment on this run-down Victorian with good bones in a quiet neighborhood south of downtown K.C. They'd encouraged her to dip into her savings for new appliances and updated wiring. They'd set her up on a couple of dates and said they understood when Elise bowed out of seeing those perfectly nice men a second or third time.

It was just her and Spike and a lot of hard work now. Hardly her dream life. Quinn and his wife were raising a family, all right, but Elise wasn't any part of it. After Quinn and Nikolai, she didn't want a man in her life. It hurt too much to love the wrong person, to believe in something that wasn't really hers. She couldn't trust a strong shoulder to lean on, even if it did smell of crisp cotton and musky man.

An image of George Madigan's stern countenance drifted into her thoughts. Turning to him for grounding comfort had been so tempting this afternoon. A full-fledged smile from the man would probably awaken the hormones she kept in careful stasis inside her. And she could guess that a man in the prime of his life like George would definitely know how to use that firm, masculine mouth to kiss a woman.

"Really?" Alarmed by the sudden drift of her thoughts, Elise put the glass to her own lips, mentally warning herself to chill. She knew the hazards of a workplace romance better than anyone.

She shouldn't wish that she had more hugs and laughter and love in her life. She had her job at KCPD and her own place that was gradually transforming into a thing of beauty. George needed her to keep his life and office running efficiently, not speculate about kissing him. After a hundred years of use and neglect, this house needed her to care for it. Her days were full. Both jobs were as rewarding as they were exhausting. She'd adopted a wonderful dog from a shelter to keep her company. She didn't have to depend on anyone. She didn't need anything more.

She shouldn't want...more.

A drop of ice-cold water fell from the glass and splashed her thigh near the fraying hem of her denim shorts, startling her from the depressing quagmire of her thoughts. "Oh. Wow."

She hadn't gone to that dark place for a while, and hated that she'd allowed the loneliness to creep into her head the moment she'd stopped for a break. Must be the flowers she'd received at work and deposited at St. Luke's Medical Center afterward for distribution to needy patients. The gift reminded her of that horrible time, that was all. It didn't mean she still had to wallow in the past.

Dismissing any remnants of longing or dissatisfaction, Elise wiped away the rivulet of water on her skin and swallowed the last of her tea. Swinging her feet down to the deck, she sat up on the edge of the chaise lounge and peered over the railing to find the dog before heading inside. "Spike?"

Just as she put her lips together to whistle, he let out a high-pitched bark and charged through the yard, heedless of the spinning water that dampened his hair as he ran past. He was sounding the toodle alarm, barking at something or someone at the side of the house.

Elise set down her glass and stood. "Spike! Shush!" With the last fingers of daylight leaving the high, cloudless sky a muted shade of gray, she could guess it was around nine o'clock.

Some of her older neighbors were probably trying to settle in for the night. "You'll wake someone." She clapped her hands to divert his attention. "Spike!"

But fifteen pounds of ferocious guard dog wouldn't be silenced.

Elise hurried down the steps and followed him to the chain-link fence to see what had alarmed him. But when she saw the tall blond man walking up the sidewalk to her backyard gate, she slowed her steps. Her guest might look handsome enough in his pressed jeans and polo shirt, but he wasn't necessarily welcome. "James."

"Is it safe?" James Westbrook tucked the skinny sack he carried beneath one arm and knelt down to hold his hand flat against the fence to let Spike sniff and lick his palm. "Hey, big guy. Remember me?" Spike's barking quieted with the recognition of a familiar scent. But his long tail curled between his legs and he darted behind Elise when James reached over the top of the gate to pet him. "I guess not."

As he pulled back to his side of the gate, Elise brushed her hair off her forehead, although that was probably the least messy thing about her ratty painting attire. She noted with annoyance that James's well-gelled hair was barely moving in the bursts of wind swirling dust and dirt through the air. "What are you doing here? It's late."

"I rang the doorbell, but no one answered."

Elise glanced up at the steady hum of her bedroom air conditioner, sticking out from the window above the back door. She hadn't heard anything. Of course, the sprinkler made a little bit of noise. And she'd been neck deep in self-pity for the past few minutes, too.

But wouldn't Spike have heard the doorbell? Or the slam of a car door? Maybe that's what had alerted him in the first place. If so, James had decided pretty quickly to come to the back-yard rather than wait on the porch for her to answer.

Despite the ninety-degree heat that lingered, Elise shivered with an uncomfortable sense of déjà vu. Since the debacle of Nikolai, she never had liked surprises. And now she'd had two in the same day? She tipped her chin up to assess James's unexpected arrival. "What are you doing here?" she repeated. "You got my message, didn't you?"

"That you were working late?" He adjusted the slim glasses he wore and smiled. "I thought you meant at the office. If I'd known you were painting tonight, I'd have gotten some takeout and come over to help." He glanced down at the gate between them, then pulled off the sack to reveal the bottle of wine he'd brought. "May I come in? It's a cabernet sauvignon, like we drank back at Mizzou."

Another gift.

Perhaps not as significant as twenty-three roses, but unsettling, all the same.

"James," she began. Elise inhaled a deep breath, clearing the *Go away* from the tip of her tongue and summoning a polite explanation. Not that she really owed him one. But bitchiness just wasn't in her nature. "I did work until about six. Then I had errands to run. By the time I got home, it was too late to meet you anywhere. So I changed into these old clothes, zapped some leftovers in the microwave and went to work on the shutters."

"What do you do for fun, Lise?"

Trying not to bristle at the pet name he'd given her when they'd been dating, Elise gestured toward the pale gray siding and white trim. "Reclaiming this house is fun for me."

"No. That's rewarding," he corrected with a teasing smile. "Sounds like you're avoiding me." He raised the wine bottle again. "Could be why I felt like I needed to bring a peace offering."

Guilty feelings surfaced, then eased out on a

breathy sigh. "It's not you, James," she assured him. "It's me." And a screwed-up love life, a little lack of confidence and nary a spark of the attraction a younger, more innocent Elise had once felt for him. "I'm flattered by your attention, but I'm just not interested in a relationship right now."

"I get that." He dropped his hand to the gate, but she still made no move to open it. "You and I broke up a long time ago when we graduated from college and I took that job in Korea. But we're still friends, right? We share history. I've been back in the States for a couple of months now, but Kansas City doesn't feel like home yet. I find I'm still thinking in a foreign language. I make wrong turns in the neighborhood where I grew up. Landmarks have changed or aren't even there anymore." He slid his hand over to rest on hers. "Can you blame me for seeking out a familiar face?"

Elise pulled away from the warmth of his fingers and bent down to pick up the dog. It was an obvious wall of defense she was putting up, but Spike didn't seem to mind. The dog licked her jaw a couple of times before settling into her arms and Elise smiled, even as James's faded. "What about your father?" she asked. "Isn't he retired now? Won't he spend time with you? There's a Royals game on TV tonight."

"To be honest, I was hoping for some younger, prettier company than Dad. You and I could watch the game." He slipped the wine bottle back into the sack and held it out to her. "I promise to keep the evening perfectly platonic."

The streetlamp in front of her house flickered on and grew bright. Even if she trusted James's promise, the hour was late. She had to be at work early in the morning. "To be honest, I was getting ready to clean up and go to bed."

His eyes narrowed behind his glasses before he sighed and shook his head. "Once upon a time you and I talked about getting married, Lise."

The regret in his tone cooled the air around them. She'd admit that there were some good memories between them. But that was all they were—memories. There was not one pang of hope or regret when she looked at James now. "We were practically kids then. You wanted to see the world, and I'd snagged that internship at Gallagher Security Systems. We just weren't meant to be."

"You turned that internship at GSS into a career, didn't you. I bet you were making good money there." He folded his arms over his chest, eyeing her like the businessman he was. "Why'd you leave that kind of success and take a job with the city?"

Her smile faded. She rubbed her fingers along the soft warmth of Spike's flank, buying time to compose herself before deciding on the appropriate answer. She wound up using the same vague truth she'd given in her interview with George Madigan. "Money isn't everything. There was nothing more for me at GSS. I wanted new surroundings. I needed a new challenge."

"Turning this into a showplace isn't challenging enough?" He pointed to the painter's tape lining the glass inside the dining room windows. "Are you sure I can't help you do something here?"

Elise looked at his hands, which were pale and pristine compared to the stained fingers with which she was petting the dog. He wasn't really into home repair work, was he? "I've made enough of a mess for one night. I'm really tired."

"Maybe another time?" He put up his hands in placating surrender before she could answer. "Strictly as friends. I don't know why you're so gun-shy about rekindling things, but I won't put any pressure on you. Like I said, I'm just looking for someone my age to hang out with until I get my feet under me again."

"How about I invite you over the next time I have a big piece of furniture to move."

He laughed, and the awkwardness between them eased a little bit. "Deal." He thrust the wine over the top of the gate. "Here. You'd better take this."

Elise backed away a step. "I couldn't."

"Of course, you can. It's a gift."

If he was hoping she'd invite him in to share a glass, then he'd be in for a long wait. Still, she sensed he wasn't going to move until she accepted the so-called peace offering. At least she knew who was giving her this gift. She wrapped her hand around the neck of the bottle.

"Thank you." *Ask him. Why not?* Clearing up the mystery would go a long way toward improving her chances of getting a good night's sleep. "Did you send me flowers at work today? There wasn't a card attached, and the officer at the front desk said he didn't find one, either. I haven't had a chance to check with the florist yet. It's a bit of a mystery."

"You used to like it when I sent you flowers." He grinned. "Remember? A daisy or a rose? To commemorate any little event—acing an exam, the start of spring break…" He grasped the rail at the top of the gate and leaned in. "Thanking you for a special night?"

Yes. Those had been sweet and romantic and fitting for the young couple they'd once been. Not the point. "The flowers I got today weren't cheap."

He snorted. "That cabernet wasn't cheap."

"James, did you—?"

"I can see I'm not getting anywhere with you tonight." He shook his head, then adjusted his glasses, glancing skyward before zeroing his gaze in on hers. "Keep an eye on the weather. We're under a tornado watch until midnight. I wouldn't want you or the pooch there to get hurt. Good night."

And then he was striding away.

Her mouth opened to call after him to clarify his response to her question, but Elise wisely snapped it shut. Better to just let him leave. "Good night," she muttered.

Were straight answers really so much to ask for? Elise plopped Spike down on his feet in the grass as James walked to the curb where he'd parked. A black-and-white police car cruised past on its regular rounds for the night, giving her ex the impetus to climb behind the wheel and start the engine when he hesitated at the open door, no doubt readying another argument as to why she should rethink sending him away.

Elise waited for James to pull into the driveway behind her car and back out in the opposite direction to leave the neighborhood, and then she turned off the water and picked up her glass. "Come on, boy. Here, Spike."

The dog bounded up onto the deck and followed her into the house. He danced around her feet while she locked the back door and headed into the kitchen. She hit the light switch with her elbow, flooding the room with light before setting the wine on the granite counter and rinsing out her glass. She turned on the radio to get an update on the possibility of dangerous weather, got Spike a treat from the jar next to the sink and set about her nightly check of the doors and windows on the first floor.

She secured locks and pulled window shades and makeshift curtains, listening to the jingle of Spike's tags as he lapped up a drink of water in the kitchen. She stopped for several seconds in front of the living room air conditioner, unhooking the top couple of buttons on her paint shirt and cooling the perspiration on her skin before turning it down for the night. Moving into the foyer, the growing noise from the wind cruising through the leafy trees outside and knocking twigs and other debris against the house fully registered. Elise paused with her fingers on the front door's dead bolt.

She could hear the dog in the kitchen at the back of the house.

Her breath hitched in her chest at the disquieting thought that crossed her mind. Praying that she'd be proved wrong, Elise quickly returned to the living room and turned the AC unit back on high. The light in the foyer flickered at the sudden drain on the neighborhood's overtaxed power grid as the machine roared to life and the cold air blasted her again.

Noisy enough. She couldn't hear Spike anymore.

Then she opened the red front door and reached outside to press the doorbell.

The instant the bell chimed, Spike barked and came running from the kitchen. He barked again, eager to greet or warn off their visitor.

"Shush. It's okay, sweetie. It's just Mommy testing a theory."

But the yapping and squealing continued until she picked him up and pushed open the storm door to show him no one was there. Greeted by a wall of summer heat and uncomfortable suspicion, Elise crossed the porch, mentally timing how long it took her to reach the railing at the edge of the house.

Elise hugged the dog against her shoulder, patting his back as if burping a baby. "He lied to us, Spike."

Such a small slip of the tongue. Maybe nothing more sinister than a clichéd response.

I rang the doorbell.

No way had James stood on her front porch, announcing his arrival. He would have needed to sprint down the steps and around the side of the house to the back gate to reach her before Spike heard the bell and sounded his alarm. But James had strolled up the walk. His breathing had been perfectly normal, without a drop of sweat visible anywhere.

Glancing up and down the street, Elise peered into shadows beyond the streetlights but saw nothing out of sorts. The only thing that wasn't right was the portentous wind that made her clothes instantly stick to her skin again, and the nagging suspicion about a man who claimed to be her friend.

Why would James lie? What was the point of sneaking around her house? And when she'd asked him about the flowers, he'd never actually confirmed sending them. Or denied it.

She'd gotten rid of the roses. She'd gotten rid of James.

But she couldn't get rid of the feeling that her life had taken a very weird, very unsettling turn.

GEORGE HEARD THE hurried rhythm of a woman's high heels tapping across KCPD headquarters' marble floors behind him.

"Hold the elevator, please."

Even if he hadn't recognized the voice, he would have pushed the button to hold the doors open. It was the polite thing to do. But he did recognize Elise Brown's articulate, slightly breathless tone, and his blood suffused with an instant warmth.

"Thanks." Elise tilted her head and smiled as she darted into the car and moved to the railing behind him.

He knew it was wrong to identify his assistant by the warm contralto pitch of her voice. And he shouldn't be familiar with the faint whiff of tropical fruits that emanated from the soft waves of her chin-length hair as she breezed past him. His gaze dipped down to the navy blue heels she wore without hose, a choice made in deference to the forecasted triple-digit temperatures, no doubt. While a part of him admired the sensible concession to the summer heat wave, George's chest constricted and he resolutely averted his eyes.

He wasn't admiring her sensibility. He was imprinting the curve of her smooth, tanned calves beneath a hemline that brushed the top of her knees to memory, coming up with another completely inappropriate, equally unmistakable way to identify Elise Brown.

Yeah, his life would be a heck of a lot easier if he wasn't so observant of little details like that—especially where his executive assistant was concerned.

Pushing the button for the eighth floor, George tempered the quickened pace of his breathing and made sure his commander-in-chief expression was in place before he turned to greet her. "Good morning, Elise."

He might have hit fifty, but he wasn't dead. He was single and he was a man. Couldn't blame a guy for noticing an attractive woman. Still, it wasn't quite protocol to charge up with this rush of energy just because she'd smiled at him, just because he got to spend a few moments alone on the elevator with her clean, fresh scent. He felt more awake, more alert, than he had a few seconds ago. And he hadn't even had his first cup of coffee yet.

She tucked her sunglasses into the modest

neckline of her sleeveless dress and brushed a swath of nut-brown hair off her cheek. "Good morning, sir."

Way to kill the buzz. It was one thing for the men and women he outranked at KCPD to refer to him with the respectful title. It was something else again for the woman he worked with every day of his life to call him sir. Hearing that from Elise, no matter how well intended, always made him feel like one of her father's friends or a Dutch uncle. It was easy to squash any perky urge to smile now.

The doors drifted together and the elevator made a slight bounce before starting its ascent. "It's George, remember?"

"I'm sorry. Good morning, George."

"No need to apologize. I'll just keep reminding you until you get it right," he teased.

Only, she didn't seem to get the joke. Her blue gaze darted up to his before she suddenly needed something from her flowered purse and focused her attention there. "Of course."

While he was careful about crossing the line into anything that could be construed as sexual harassment, there was no harm in being friends. Yet Elise seemed to shoot down every overture of appreciation or concern that could take them to being more than polite acquaintances who shared the same connected office space.

Even yesterday afternoon, when the delivery of those flowers had clearly upset her, she hadn't opened up one bit. Maybe a small stab of unprofessional jealousy had made him linger in her office longer than he'd intended. She'd lit up at first, once she found out the bouquet was meant for her, and he'd been curious enough to find out what kind of man she was dating who could turn her serious, practical head like that.

But even when Elise's smile had changed to a frown, and her troubled thoughts had been written on her face, she hadn't been interested in sharing a thing. She hadn't even wanted him to dust off his rusty investigative skills and make a few quick inquiries to find where the bouquet had come from for her.

The elevator continued its familiar climb, but there was little familiar about Elise's oddly distracted behavior this morning. She pulled a ring of keys and fobs from her bag and clutched them in her fist, staring at them. Tugging back the front of his suit jacket, George propped his hands at his waist. "Is everything all right?"

"What?" Her eyes locked on to his, telling him one thing before she stuffed the keys back into her purse and told him something else. "Oh.

I couldn't find the spare key I leave on my front porch after I walked the dog this morning." She patted her purse. "I like to use it so I don't have to carry all these and be weighed down. Don't worry. We got in through the keypad by the garage door. That's why I'm running a little late today."

Uh-uh. She wasn't dismissing the confusion he'd read in her gaze. Not this time. "Are you worried someone stole the key?"

The corners of her mouth tightened as she fixed the smile on her lips. "I probably locked it inside the house the last time I used it and forgot. I didn't have much time to look."

George valued Elise as his assistant. His office had been a chaotic mess after the previous assistant retired. Elise had come in, quickly grasping the old information management and communication systems and updating them in ways that made his job easier, and made the entire deputy commissioner's office a model of professional efficiency that other administrative departments were now copying.

But he'd been friends with each of his partners over the years. He'd gotten to know officers and staff alike. He knew the names of their children; whether they were football, baseball or basketball fans, or if they were even into sports at all. He knew what their favorite places to eat were and what issues they might be struggling with on the job or off the clock.

Elise went to great lengths to keep her personal life out of the office. He knew the names of her parents from her personnel file, but had never met them. And other than noting she wore no wedding ring and kept no pictures except one of a small black poodle on her desk, he couldn't confirm whether or not she was in a relationship with anyone.

As stormy as his marriage to Courtney had been, he'd always kept a memento of her on his desk or in his wallet. And now that they were divorced, he had family pictures from his nephew Nick's wedding on the shelves in his office, as well as a group photo from his twenty-fifth reunion at the University of Central Missouri on his desk.

But Elise? No pictures. No personal touches. Just the dog in her lap in one five-by-seven photo, and an invisible wall that said *Keep Out*.

George butted in, anyway. "Something's upset you again. Something more than a misplaced key." He shifted his stance, feeling the elevator slow its ascent. "What is it?"

For a few endless seconds, she tilted her cornflower-blue eyes up to his, giving him a glimpse of the turbulent emotions darkening their depths. Feeling an instinctive urge to respond to that unspoken plea for help, George stepped closer and reached for her.

But the elevator jerked to a stop. Elise blinked her gaze from his and moved to the front of the car. "I'm okay," she lied.

The doors slid open and the chance to help was lost.

A lanky cop with dark blond hair that needed to see a comb rose from his chair behind the eighth floor security desk to greet them. "Good morning, sir. Morning, Elise."

"Wilkins." George slipped his hands into the pockets of his slacks, not sure what to do with the fingertips that itched with frustrated anticipation at the interrupted moment on the elevator.

Elise hurried across the lobby ahead of him to swipe her ID badge over the computerized card reader that Officer Wilkins set on top of the desk. Her serene smile was firmly in place as she looped the ID lanyard around her neck. "Hey, Shane. How are you today?"

The young uniformed officer hooked his thumbs into his utility belt and pulled his shoulders back. "Fit and fine. Ran my five miles this morning."

"In this heat?"

Shane laughed. "That's why I do it before dawn. No matter what the weather does to us, I have to stick to my training if I'm going to place in KC's half marathon on Labor Day weekend. It's only a few weeks away."

Elise gave an exaggerated groan. "I barely want to walk out to my car in this heat. I admire your persistence and dedication."

The younger man winked at her. "I try."

George swiped his card and then clipped it to his belt beside his badge. He was out of smiles this morning and ready to work. "Is Commissioner Cartwright-Masterson in yet?"

Shane rightly turned his attention to his superior officer. "No, sir. Do you want me to tell her you're looking for her when she checks in?"

George shook his head, hating that he was in such a mood. "No. I'm just curious if there's any news on her son Seth's baby yet. I know she wants to take a few days off then, but I'm hoping to get a little heads-up before it happens and the extra workload kicks in."

"If I hear anything, you will, too," Shane assured him.

"Thanks." Elise was already heading around the corner into the hallway that led to their offices. Running away from him and his questions, it seemed. Whatever she'd been about to share in the elevator had been locked up tight inside her again. He'd be a smart man to respect her privacy and forget his concern. He'd be a smarter man to take care of the people he was responsible for. He flattened his hand on top of the counter, demanding Shane's undivided attention. "In between screening visitors, you ought to apply some of that 'persistence and dedication' to studying for your detective's exam. You got your degree in May, right?"

"Yes, sir. Finished it in three years instead of four. And that's while I was working full-time."

With that kind of drive, Shane was probably frustrated getting stuck on guard duty at KCPD headquarters. "You know I'll put in a good word for you with the promotions board as soon as you pass the exam."

"I appreciate that."

George nodded. Sometimes, it was nice to have clout and be able to make a difference in a deserving person's life. "Have a good one."

"You, too, sir."

And sometimes that clout didn't do him a damn bit of good. George followed Elise to the reception area and the suite of offices at the end of the hallway. When he nudged open the door to her office, he was instantly hit with the sickeningly sweet smell of roses filling the air. And in the split second he wondered if a woman really was impressed with that stinky kind of excess, he plowed into Elise's back.

"Whoa." Before he sent her flying across the carpet, George grabbed her by the shoulders and kept her from falling. "Is there a reason why you stopped in the middle of the room?"

"They shouldn't be here."

And that's when he realized she was frozen. In more ways than one. Her upper arms felt like ice beneath his fingers. He couldn't seem to help rubbing his hands up and down her chilled skin, trying to instill some warmth. He looked over her shoulder to her desk and the yellow roses that had transfixed her, and this time, he wasn't budging until he got an answer. "Explain."

Elise never averted her gaze, never took a step away from him, so George never let go. She eased a sigh out on a deep, stuttered breath, then inhaled again before answering.

"It bothered me that I didn't know who sent the roses, so I dropped them off at St. Luke's on the way home last night. They're too much and I didn't want them." She hugged her arms in front of her and shivered in his grip. "I got rid of them."

George stepped up beside her to get a better

look, dropping a steadying hand to the small of her back. "You're certain these are the same?"

She nodded, recoiling a bit against his palm. "Cut-glass vase. There are only twenty-three roses, not twenty-four. One stem is broken. He brought them back."

George quickly verified her description and began formulating possible scenarios to explain this twisted prank. Judging by her behavior in the elevator, he could guess this wasn't the only worrisome puzzle Elise had been dealing with.

But how much of the story was she willing to share? How hard would he have to push her to get to the truth? And were her troubles any of his damn business?

Yes.

This was a threat to his office. A breach of security at the highest ranks of the police department. Besides, seeing cool, calm and collected Elise Brown rattled like this—to see his right arm, his executive partner being hurt this way—felt personal. They were a team. And nobody messed with his teammates. He'd had his partners' backs for years when he'd worn a uniform or cleaned drugs and thugs off the streets. Even though his gun was locked in his desk drawer, he was still a cop. He couldn't allow this kind of thing to happen in his office, not on his watch. Not to Elise.

"I'll take care of it," he said, turning her back out of her office. The fact that she didn't argue with him was as much of a red flag as the creepy reappearance of the bouquet. Something was seriously wrong here.

George led her to a couch in the reception area before marching down the hall to have Shane get a list of everyone who'd been on this floor in the past twelve hours, as well as any cleaning and maintenance staff or personnel who had master keys. He'd make sure every last one was accounted for. He'd make this right.

Or else he'd never be able to shake the memory of Elise trembling against the palm of his hand and murmuring to herself, "He brought them back."

Chapter Three

Missing keys. Unwanted gifts. Unanswered questions.

Elise was beginning to wonder if someone was trying to gaslight her into thinking she was nuts. Or maybe she really was going crazy.

George had removed the flowers before she reentered her office that morning. And though she was curious to know what he'd done with them, she was more relieved to have them gone.

He'd made a couple of calls on his cell phone. No one at the medical center remembered seeing her the night before. And the clerk at the information desk said she'd handled too many deliveries to recall any one particular bouquet of roses.

Elise watched George pace in and out of their office suite, keeping an eye on her and warning her to stay put, even after she'd come to her senses, reined in the fearful paranoia and assured him she was fit for duty. She was nearly an hour behind brewing coffee and sending out the daily correspondence before George and Annie Fensom, a petite, dark-haired woman from the crime lab, exited Elise's office and her boss had declared she could go in.

Although Elise recognized Annie from the wedding photos in George's office, she knew the CSI hadn't answered his call to take care of family business. She'd come with her lab kit and left with a kiss on the cheek from her uncle-in-law and a promise to try to identify the "numerous prints" she'd found in and around Elise's desk. Not that Annie was holding out much hope, she'd overheard. There were no fingerprints on the vase itself, not even Elise's, indicating the glass had been wiped clean. And any prints around the room could be attributed to the KCPD personnel, maintenance staff and registered guests who came in and out of the office on a regular basis.

The deputy commissioner had ordered Shane to bring her a bottle of water, and then put him to work compiling a list of everyone who'd been on this floor between the time they'd closed up shop the evening before and when Shane had reported for duty this morning. Shane had offered to make a second list of anyone in maintenance or other departments who had keys to access the building offices, earning him some brownie points with the deputy commissioner for his thorough thinking.

While she was glad George had been there to keep her sane and upright when she might have done something stupid like burst into tears or hurl the vase out the window to the sidewalk below, Elise knew it was important to renew her independence and resurrect the emotional walls that kept her boss at an impersonal distance again. She wouldn't turn over her trust to a man simply because she needed someone, the way she had with Nikolai. And she couldn't sit around and do nothing while everyone else around her worked—especially when it was her problem they were trying to solve.

It had taken two friendly assurances, and finally a third "Go" that was a little more terse, to convince George to leave for his lunch meeting.

Frankly, Elise was glad to have an hour of quiet while she ate her lunch at her desk and got her day back on schedule and her head back where it needed to be. She'd already sent out two memos with the wrong date this morning before she caught her mistake. Not that being a day off would cause anyone any grief, but the police department prided itself on getting their facts straight, and, as a representative of KCPD, so did she.

Quiet. Focus. Normal routine. Those were the things she needed to get her day back on track.

Quiet, she'd managed by staying in the office instead of joining her coworkers in the break room. Typing and filing and organizing were about as routine as her job could get.

But focus? Elise had turned on a small fan to disperse the lingering odor of the roses that had filled the room, but she was having a harder time dispelling the clean, masculine scent of George Madigan that seemed to permeate every inch of carpeting and upholstery in the adjoining rooms. Or maybe his was just a unique fragrance that had burned into her memory when she'd leaned into him this morning.

She could rationalize that the remembered scent was a mental association that had to do with strength and security. Thinking of her boss as a man who made her feel safe was perfectly reasonable. But there was nothing rational about wishing she could burrow into that heat and strength and enticing scent, and simply forget about the weird happenings of the past two days. If she wasn't careful, that need to feel safe, that latent awareness of an attractive man, might blossom into an emotional connection, into those feelings of trust and desire that had been her downfall more than once in her life.

Elise drank a long sip of iced tea through her straw and wished she'd opted for hot coffee so that the strong smell of brewed java could drown out the imagined scent of George Madigan that lingered in her nose. No matter. By sheer strength of will, she would override her hormones and emotions and concentrate on the job at hand. She needed nothing more, and she wanted nothing less. Right?

"Right."

Popping a baby carrot into her mouth, Elise printed off the draft of the speech she'd typed for her boss and stood to pick up the papers from the printer on the credenza beneath the window. She swallowed the carrot and crunched her way through another before sliding the speech into the folder she'd prepared and carrying it into George's office.

Elise studiously ignored the picture of George and his sister's family behind his desk as she set the file on the blotter. But after seeing her just a few hours earlier, Annie Fensom's wedding gown drew Elise's eye. The CSI and George's nephew, Nick Fensom, made a striking couple with their dark hair against the lacy white gown and gray tuxedoes adorned with bright red boutonnieres.

But it was the distinguished-looking man standing behind the groom and his mother that kept Elise's attention. She'd walked by those pictures dozens of times every day for the past few months. How had she never noticed that before? She reached out and touched her fingertip to the glass over George Madigan's face. "You're smiling."

Without even thinking, Elise smiled, too. The relaxed expression on George's face was so compelling, so rare, that she wondered just what it would take to see that handsome grin again.

But just as quickly as the intriguing challenge registered, Elise pressed her lips into a frown. "Idiot."

Would she never learn her lesson?

The telephone on George's desk rang, startling her. A word cursing her own foolishness slipped out before she picked up the receiver. "Deputy Commissioner Madigan's office," she snapped.

"Elise?"

Every raw emotion and dangerous thought in Elise's head short-circuited at the familiar tenor of the caller's masculine voice. "Mr. Gallagher."

"Really?" She heard a wry laugh. "You haven't called me that since the first day you worked for me. Don't tell me George or KCPD is insisting on that kind of formality." Quinn Gallagher, a wealthy inventor and the CEO of Gallagher Security Systems, was teasing her. "You and I are old friends."

Friends. Right. Her heart had been far too slow to understand that little distinction in their once close relationship. Funny how talking to the man she'd loved and lost could turn her light lunch into a rock at the pit of her stomach. Still, she'd moved on with her life. And, if nothing else, she prided herself on being the quintessential professional. "Hi, Quinn," she answered with a rueful smile. "How are you?"

"Happier than I've been in a long time."

"How's Miranda?" she forced herself to ask.

"Still can't get that woman to cook a decent meal. I thought when she got pregnant some kind of natural domestic instinct would kick in." He sounded younger, energized, blissfully content, as he always did when he talked about his wife and daughter. "Fortunately, she knows all the best take-out places, and she and Fiona have been setting up picnics on the living room floor this past week."

Any pangs of jealousy Elise felt were beaten back by the guilt of knowing she'd nearly cost her former boss this second chance at love and the family he was enjoying now. "Sounds like fun."

"How are you?" Quinn asked.

"Loving my work," she answered honestly. "And the house is halfway done. The kitchen and bathrooms have been redone and the exterior is all painted."

"I know that house is your therapy, but I wish I could tear you away from it. Are you sure a raise wouldn't convince you to come back to GSS?" His generous salary had enabled her to afford the extensive remodel in the first place. "I'm still having a hard time breaking in my new assistant. Working with you was so easy. I think you could read my mind. You spoiled me for anyone else."

"You're too kind, Quinn." But their working relationship had never been the problem between them. "The commissioner's out at a lunch meeting. May I take a message?"

Quinn's teasing tone sobered. "This is a subject I'd rather discuss in person. Soon, if George has got a half hour for me in his schedule."

Elise clicked the mouse on George's desk and pulled up his appointment calendar on the computer screen. "What should I tell him it's regarding?"

"Alexsandr Titov."

Her legs turned to jelly at the unexpected answer, and Elise sank into the plush leather chair behind George's desk. "Nikolai's brother?"

"The same. Did you ever meet him?"

"Only over the phone." Alexsandr had called her from Lukinburg, the night of Nikolai's murder. *What can you tell me about my brother's death? Did your jealous husband do this to him?* Apparently, he'd found her name on a hotel receipt in Nikolai's bloody jacket pocket. For a moment, Elise couldn't catch her breath. "It was a brief chat."

And not a particularly friendly one.

Quinn continued, "Since you knew Nikolai, you may want to sit in on this meeting, too."

"Me? Why?"

"Alexsandr is here in Kansas City, according to my sources. Staying in a hotel downtown near Embassy Row."

Only a few miles from this very office. She had no husband. She'd had nothing to do with Nikolai's death. Still, the news of Alexsandr Titov setting foot on Missouri soil felt like a threat. "Do you know why he's here?"

Words like *payback* and *revenge* came to mind.

Quinn laughed, but there was no humor. "That's the million-dollar question. Since Nikolai's death, his younger brother, Alexsandr, has been rebuilding Titov Industrial. He's had pretty good success selling military rifles and ammunition in the Far East. Kansas City is a big import/export area. He could be here legitimately, trying to expand his business."

The words on the computer monitor had blurred. Elise blinked them back into focus and searched for a free block of time on George's calendar. "Or he could be as big a criminal as Nikolai was."

"Exactly why I want to give George and KCPD a heads-up. Since he handles equipment and munitions purchases for the department, I wanted to make sure he isn't spending any money on a dummy corporation that's laundering money or selling arms illegally the way his brother did. And..." Quinn paused again.

"What?"

"The deputy commissioner has a perfectly legitimate reason for investigating Titov Industrial as a potential resource. I want to know if Alexsandr's visit has anything to do with Nikolai's death."

Guilt stabbed through Elise. "Your father-in-law killed him."

"Vasily might have used his mob connections to eliminate Nikolai after he tried to kill my daughter and destroy GSS. But you and I both know that Nikolai's hate ran pretty deep. He blamed me for his business going under and his son's death. And he turned you into an unwitting mole." Until she came to her senses and gave testimony to the police and FBI that helped get Nikolai deported back to Lukinburg…and a waiting assassin. "I don't know if it's the same for his younger brother or not. Like I said, he could be in the KC area for legitimate business reasons."

She'd never met Nikolai's younger brother, but if one Titov could break the law and take advantage of a heartsick woman to gain access to procedure codes and personnel files, it wasn't a stretch of the imagination to believe another Titov would be willing to terrorize her or use her for some nefarious purpose.

Maybe he'd send twenty-three roses just like Nikolai had.

Or steal the key to a woman's house.

Guilt wasn't the only emotion churning through Elise's stomach now.

She pulled the receiver from her mouth to muffle her strangled gasp. Was Alexsandr plotting something to make her pay for his brother's death? Or was this yet another creepy coincidence her suspicious imagination was turning into something more dangerous and disturbing than it really was?

"Elise?"

With too many questions and no answers, and no one to calm her fears, Elise went back to the one thing that had never failed her. Work. Tucking the receiver between her shoulder and ear, she typed Quinn's name into the computer. "Would tomorrow morning work for you?"

"That'll be fine. See you then."

Elise replaced the receiver in the phone cradle, holding on until she heard the voices in the other room. She pushed the chair back from the desk and stood, but not before George Madigan filled the open doorway.

"What's wrong?"

Stone-gray eyes locked on to hers, and Elise nearly answered the concern written there.

But the shrill voice of common sense interrupted before she gave in to temptation.

"It's not as if I'm asking you to do this for a stranger." The curvy blonde who made frequent appearances in the deputy commissioner's office nudged George aside and walked into the room. She picked up a file folder from the desk and, after an exasperated sigh, fanned herself with it. "Ken Biro was your partner. You'd think you could help with a simple birthday party."

"Good afternoon, Mrs. Mad—Ms. Reiter." Elise corrected her greeting to the boss's ex-wife, tipped her chin to a relatively confident angle and crossed the room to return to her desk. "Quinn Gallagher just made an appointment for tomorrow morning to discuss Titov Industrial and potential munitions contracts with the city," she reported to George. "I marked your calendar. I'll bring in the file with the negotiations transcripts to review for your two o'clock. The retirement banquet speech is on your desk."

Elise quickly slipped by him out the door, but he grabbed her hand as she passed, forcing her to stop and turn. George's steely eyes silently demanded an explanation, but it was the warm brush of his thumb across her knuckles that almost had her spilling the details about her connection to Alexsandr Titov and the potential threat he represented.

"Good afternoon, Elise." Courtney Reiter's gaze had zeroed in on the clasp of hands between boss and assistant.

Telling herself she was glad for the blonde's dismissive tone, Elise snatched her hand away and hurried back to her desk.

Muttering a curse beneath his breath, George strode into his office. He plucked the file from his ex-wife's grasp and set it back on the desk. "I thought this conversation was over, Court. You never even liked Ken. Why is this such a big deal?"

Courtney's voice grew louder as she approached the door. "Ken has been a part of our lives for years. Just because we fight like cats and dogs on occasion doesn't mean he isn't my friend, too. In fact..." The blonde waited for Elise to look her way before she smiled sweetly...and closed the door.

Well, that message was clear as crystal. *Stay out of my business.* Though whether the older woman's warning stemmed from an arrogance that relegated Elise to being the hired help who needed to remember her place, or a more possessive streak of jealousy at seeing George and Elise holding hands, was less clear.

The click of the door left Elise feeling chilled and alone. Could Alexsandr Titov really blame her for his brother's murder? After all, she'd been Nikolai's victim. He'd swept her off her feet and she'd fancied herself in love with him. She'd even slept with him because she'd been that desperately lonely and he seemed to care. But once she found out how he'd used her to gain inside information on Quinn Gallagher and

GSS, she'd willingly labeled him a criminal and provided a deposition against him.

What would she have done if Courtney Reiter hadn't laid claim to George's time and attention? Would Elise have turned into that broad chest? Spilled her guts? Confessed how a previously unacknowledged, forbidden attraction had simmered to the surface with the intensity of the summer heat wave?

Elise folded her hands together in her lap and rubbed the spot where George had held her. The firm clasp of fingers. The gentle stroke of his thumb. She could still feel his touch on her skin. She could vividly remember those brief moments of being sheltered, cared for. She could see herself wanting, needing, falling for the man.

"Please, George. Do this for me," Courtney pleaded on the other side of the door.

But Elise had no right to make any such demand on his time and caring. Wisely ignoring those tempting ideas, Elise put her hands on her keyboard to update the budget report. Although she didn't envy the one-sided argument she could hear through the closed door, she was relieved that George's ex-wife was demanding his attention. Let him solve Courtney's problems. Let him be a rock for someone else. Elise couldn't depend on her boss to comfort her or save her or whatever it was she thought he could do for her right now.

If she'd quit getting herself into trouble, she wouldn't need any man to save her.

Several minutes passed, long enough for Elise to get three pages of new data entered into the budget report. The uncomfortable opportunity to eavesdrop on the room next door went away as the voices quieted into a civilized conversation. George was either able to calm his ex, she was beginning to see reason or both.

Elise had managed to immerse herself in her work again when a man cleared his throat from the hallway door. Looking up, she smiled. "Officer Hale."

A quick glance at the time and the calendar confirmed the uniformed police officer was here for a scheduled appointment. "Ma'am."

She circled the desk to shake the officer's hand and gestured to the seating area of her office. "Could I get you a cup of coffee? Or something cold to drink?"

"Water if you have it." Denton Hale took a seat once Elise brought him a bottle of water from the minifridge and sat. Although his short-sleeved uniform was neatly pressed, the dark marks at his armpits indicated he was taking a

break in the middle of a work shift. He opened
the bottle and drank half of it before capping it
and thanking her. "That hit the spot. My partner
and I recently got our shift transferred to your
neighborhood. At least I think it's your part of
town—I saw you walking your dog there."

"Could be. Spike and I are out every morning and most evenings."

"The older residential districts seem to be getting hit pretty hard with brownouts and trans-
formers going off-line." The middle-aged cop
toyed with the brim of his hat, as if nervous
about coming up with more conversation. "Have
you had any power outages yet? Our electricity
went out a couple of nights ago. We all ended
up sleeping on the screened-in porch."

"That sounds like a fun adventure."

"The kids liked it, although the camp cot's a
little hard on my back these days."

Knowing Denton Hale was here to discuss
possible salary freezes and staff cuts—maybe
even his own job or that of his friends—with
the deputy commissioner, Elise did her best to
put him at ease. No sense adding to his stress.
"We've had a couple of outages, but nothing
that lasted for any length of time. I run the air-
conditioning just upstairs at night, and turn it
on low during the day—enough for my dog to

manage the heat. I'm trying to do whatever I can to help conserve energy."

"Yeah. I guess it's been pretty rough. We followed one utility worker out on a call this morning. Somebody had vandalized his work truck. Painted a message on it I wouldn't want to repeat."

Elise shook her head. "That's terrible. It's not like this weather is the city's fault. I guess tempers are shorter when the temperature is higher."

"Yes, ma'am. That's been my experience." After an awkward pause and another long drink, the police officer pointed toward George's door. "Is he in?"

Elise took his empty bottle and brought him another water. "Mr. Madigan's appointment is running a little longer than he anticipated."

Denton Hale shoved his fingers though his brown hair, finally relaxing a bit, and grinned. "I think I've had more conversations with you on this couch, waiting for the commish to talk negotiation strategies, than I have with my wife the past couple of weeks."

Elise smiled at the joke. "Budget time does that, I think. Lots of meetings, lots of waiting."

"You're easy to talk to, I guess."

"Thanks."

"I bet you're putting in extra hours, too. What does your boyfriend think of that?"

"My boyfriend?"

"A pretty lady like you must be taken." He took another drink before pointing to her. "I didn't see a ring, though."

Although she smiled, Elise suddenly wasn't feeling as welcoming as she had a moment earlier. "No boyfriend. Never married."

"That's a shame." A split second later, Officer Hale's cheeks reddened and he put up an apologetic hand. "Wait. Girlfriend?"

Shaking her head, Elise stood and checked her watch. She had no problem with small talk to make a visitor more comfortable about waiting for the deputy commissioner. But today wasn't a good day for her to be the main topic. "If you'll excuse me a moment, I'll remind Mr. Madigan that you're here."

She picked up the negotiations file from her desk and knocked softly on the black door.

"Come in."

As soon as George responded, Elise nudged open the door. He was sitting on the front edge of his desk, holding a box of tissues for his ex-wife, who was dabbing at tears. Despite a tug of sympathy, Elise quickly quashed any urge to ask if everything was okay. "Your two o'clock is here, sir. Denton Hale from the officers' union?" She handed him the file. "Here are the transcripts you wanted."

George opened the file and stood, flipping through the pages. He frowned. "You have to go now, Court. I have work to do."

"What else is new?" With another sniffle, she apologized for her sarcasm. "I'm sorry. Of course, you do. You're an important man." Courtney rose, tossed the soiled tissues into the trash and smoothed her blond hair into place. She smoothed the skirt and blouse she wore, too, before tilting her red-rimmed eyes up to George. "You're okay with this? You promise you'll help me?"

"It doesn't make much sense to me, but…" He closed the folder and nodded. "I promise. But this is it, Court. I haven't been your husband for a long time now. You've got to learn to stand on your own two feet."

"I will." Courtney Reiter stretched up onto her toes and kissed his cheek. She would have kissed his mouth if he hadn't turned his head at the last moment. "Thank you."

George groaned as if he'd heard that promise before, and wiped the pink lipstick from his skin as Courtney breezed past Elise and out the door. "We need to talk," he said to Elise, reaching around her shoulder to push the door shut behind her. He held up the folder between them. "This is the wrong file."

"What? No, I'm sure I…" She pulled it from his grip and read the label. Budget Notes. "I'm sorry. I must have grabbed the wrong one. It's a simple mistake."

"If you made mistakes, it would be. But you don't." He held the door firmly in place when she reached down to open it.

Elise held her breath, thinking it was an accident that she'd been caught in the space between the door and George's chest.

But there were no accidents with this man. He flattened his palm on the wood beside her head and leaned closer, dropping his gaze to match hers. "Talk to me. You're scaring me, Elise. I don't like it when I don't have the answers I need. Tell me what's going on. Did something else happen?."

"Something else? No, I… No." Her breath rushed out as she braced her hand on his chest to push him away. "Denton Hale is waiting. I think he's on a shift break, so I'm sure he doesn't have long. And I need to…get the transcripts."

George's skin was warm, his muscles firm beneath the crisp ecru cotton. When she felt the strong beat of his heart leaping beneath her palm, Elise realized she was doing more lingering than pushing, but couldn't seem to break away from the tempting intimacy. He probably didn't even know how all this closeness and concern was affecting her. Or maybe he did.

He covered her hand with his before she could make herself escape. His fingers splayed over hers, infusing her with warmth from both his body and touch. "We need to discuss this, too."

The quiet depth in his tone, along with his firm touch, made his message perfectly clear.

"What 'this'? There is no 'this.'" There couldn't be. Knowing he felt something, too, would only make it that much harder to keep a professional distance from him. She hugged the folder to her chest and pulled against his grip. "We're coworkers, George. Friends, at best. I respect you tremendously, and I'm grateful for the job, but you're not the kind of man I want to get involved with."

"What kind of man do you think I am?" His eyes darkened like granite and his hand fell away. "Don't answer that." Giving her the space she'd asked for, he retreated to his window overlooking the north edge of the city. "Get me the right file and show Hale in."

It was on the tip of her tongue to call him back. To tell him none of this was his fault—

to admit how easily she could fall for him. She wanted to explain her screwed-up track record with men and how her best line of defense was to avoid giving in to any of this attraction or that need. But Elise knew a smarter plan of action was to overlook the sting of his words, accept his dismissal and scoot on out of the room.

She opened the door to find Denton Hale standing next to the chair behind her desk. He'd been slightly stooped over, but pulled up as soon as he saw her. Odd. Elise crossed the room to roll her chair back into position and reclaim her personal work space. "Did you need something?"

He spun his uniform cap between his hands, nervously covering for whatever he'd been up to. "I was just trying to double-check when my appointment was. I have to report back at three."

"Sorry for the wait. The deputy commissioner will see you now."

"Dent?" George called. "Come on in."

Officer Hale's brown-eyed gaze danced over her face for a moment before he heaved a sigh. "Sorry. I know I seem a little uptight about gettin' in to see Madigan. But I need this job. My family depends on me."

Now why did that apology sound like some

kind of threat? Would she ever trust what a man said to her again? "I'm sure they do."

With a nod, he circled around her desk and closed the door as soon as the two men shook hands.

Squeezing the back of her chair as if she needed its support to stand, Elise warned herself to get a mental grip instead. She dropped the budget file onto the desk and sat down to straighten it. Yes, the appointment calendar had been moved, but so had a couple of other things. And her screen saver was no longer on, meaning Officer Hale had either bumped the mouse in his brief search, or he'd clicked it on purpose to view something on her screen. While she did keep both a written and electronic record of the deputy commissioner's appointments, the only thing on her screen was the budget report she'd been working on.

Had Denton Hale seen the paragraph about salary freezes pending evaluations for officers with poor performance reviews or reprimands in their files? Was he truly in fear of losing his job? What did Hale's service record with the department look like?

With suspicion already pumping through her blood, Elise clicked off of the report and brought up the link for KCPD service records. Just as quickly, she backed out of the system. If Denton Hale did have something in his file that targeted him for extra scrutiny and job probation or termination, it wasn't her business.

After all, she didn't want KCPD or anyone else looking too closely into her past mistakes, either.

ELISE TURNED OFF the motor of her car and reached across the seat to retrieve her purse and the pumps she'd exchanged for tennis socks and walking shoes after work.

Home. The dark red door of the gray-and-white Victorian welcomed her like a familiar sanctuary. She climbed out of her Explorer, but paused for a few moments as the hundred-degree heat and matching humidity crept over her skin, pricking open pores and sapping what energy she had left. She tilted her gaze up to the heat lightning sparking in the distant sky beyond her rooftop. There wasn't a cloud above or an answering rumble of thunder. So no break in the weather this evening.

The silent violence in the evening sky felt appropriate. Ominous and hopeless somehow. She'd become a lightning rod for suspicious people and unexplained events. She hadn't forgotten the returned roses or the missing key.

Bringing her gaze down, she studied the windows and doors, making sure nothing looked out of place. The flowers wilting on the porch needed a good soaking, but they hadn't been moved. There were no footprints in the grass, no packages left on her front steps. Maybe the key disappearing had been a fluke. As upset as she'd been with James's visit last night, she could very well have simply misplaced it and not remembered.

The only way she was truly going to know if a thief or vandal had stolen the key and broken in was to march up those steps, unlock the door herself and give the house a thorough search.

Fisting her keys in her hand and steeling herself with a resolute breath, Elise slammed the car door.

Spike barked an instant mix of excitement and welcome. Only it wasn't the muted sound of the dog announcing her arrival through the window from the back of the couch. This was louder. Clearer. Closer. What the…?

"Spike?" Elise turned toward the sound. He was outside. "Spike? Spike!"

She heard the jingle of his tags hitting together before she saw him dash around her neighbor's hedge and run to meet her.

"Spikey?" Elise dropped her shoes and

scooped him up as he leaped into her arms. She kissed his head and hugged him tight, alarmed by his panting and how hot his little body felt against her chest. "How did you get out?" She checked the rapid beat of his heart and looked into his dark brown eyes. "Are you okay, sweetie? Have you been out all day? Did I...?"

She swung her gaze toward the house. Surely she hadn't left him in the backyard in this heat. With no water? Had he climbed the fence or dug underneath it to escape? And she never let him out in the front without being on a leash. "I know I put you inside."

But she'd been out of sorts and running late this morning, so she must have forgotten him. She seemed to be forgetting a lot of things today. What was happening to her?

A lick on her earlobe, demanding more petting and less thinking, cut through Elise's confusion. She scratched his belly and tried to shake off that nagging sense that she was losing it. "It's just you and me. I'd never forget you."

Yet here he was, running through the neighborhood, waiting for her to come home.

"Come on, sweetie." She moved the toodle to one arm and bent down to pick up her pumps. She didn't care that they'd gotten scratched on the concrete. She was fighting hard to stop second-guessing herself and stay in the moment. "Let's get you something to drink."

Instead of going straight up the front steps, though, Elise carried the dog around the side of the house to the backyard. "Good."

She'd gotten at least one thing right today. The gate was still latched. She opened and closed it behind her, carrying the panting black dog up onto the deck. Pulling her keys from the outside pocket of her purse, she quickly glanced around the yard for possible escape routes. There were no holes in the dirt or gaps in the fence that were readily visible. But she'd investigate the hidden places behind the bushes and landscaping later. Right now, she needed to get Spike into the air-conditioning with a wet towel and some cool water to drink. He didn't seem bleary-eyed and shocky. Hopefully, he'd stayed in the shade or made himself at home with a friendly neighbor. But she wasn't taking any chances with her dearest companion.

Elise inserted the key into the back door, feeling another glimmer of relief to discover the knob and dead bolt were both securely locked.

Once inside, she carried Spike straight to the kitchen and set him down in front of his water bowl. While he greedily lapped up the reviving liquid, Elise set her things on the counter and turned on the faucet to wet down a kitchen towel. "Feeling better, sweetie?"

Spike nosed the food in his dish—a good sign that he wasn't feeling the ill effects of the heat, she hoped—before going back for another noisy, messy drink. Elise turned off the running water and wrung out the towel before stooping down to wrap it around the dog. "Easy—"

A loud noise banged overhead.

Spike barked a warning and lurched from her grip. But Elise grabbed him before he could get away from her. She picked him up, wet towel and all, and hugged him against her racing heart. "Spike?"

Elise looked up as the dog tipped his nose to the ceiling and barked again, a cautious little yap followed by a squeal of alarm and a high-pitched growl in his throat. It was enough of a distress signal for Elise to push to her feet. She grabbed her keys from the counter, looped her purse over her shoulder and retreated toward the back door at the sound of footsteps on the floor above her.

Footsteps running from her bedroom.

Someone was in her house.

Chapter Four

"Ma'am, I'm sorry. I just don't see any signs of forced entry." Denton Hale pointed to the television, jewelry box and smart tablet on Elise's dresser and bedside table. "And you yourself said that nothing's been taken."

Elise's head was throbbing with too much stress and a lack of food. She held herself together by hugging her arms tightly around her waist and glancing over at Spike, who was curled up next to the pillows on her bed. She schooled her patience and tucked her hair behind her ear before turning back to the uniformed officer and articulating every last word. "He was in my house. I heard him running down the stairs and out the front door."

She'd said the same thing a dozen times in the past half hour, to both Hale and his partner. She'd said it when she'd met them at the front sidewalk, said it again in every room they'd gone through together. A man was in her house.

She was certain it had been a man by the heavy tread of his step.

A man who sent her flowers and stole her key?

Or some other threat, altogether?

"You didn't get a look at this guy?" Officer Hale asked.

"No. I didn't want a confrontation with him in case he was armed or wanted to hurt me." If the man hadn't made a noise… If Spike hadn't barked… She rubbed at the goose bumps dotting her bare arms and tried to block out the horrible what-ifs swirling in the back of her mind. Harming her could very well have been what the intruder had wanted since theft didn't appear to be the motive. "I called 9-1-1 on my cell and went to the Kecks'—the retired couple next door."

"The front door was locked when we came in, Elise. May I call you that?" She didn't care. She just wanted him to believe her. "None of the locks have been tampered with, and there are no broken windows."

"So he locked it when he ran out. I told you the key was missing."

"Are you sure?" Officer Hale pulled his gloved hand from where it rested on his thick utility belt and touched her elbow. His eyebrows arched with a sympathetic smile. His tone patronized as if she was an imbecile—or a desperate woman who was making this all up to get some attention. "It's there now. You opened the box in the flowerpot and showed it to me. Remember?"

Why not just pat her on the head and say, "There, there"? Elise jerked her arm away and took a step toward her closest ally. "Spike and I both heard him."

Hale shrugged, sounding exasperated with her seeming lack of reason. "Unfortunately, I can't take the word of a fuzz mop."

Apparently, he wouldn't take her word, either. "I'm not lying. He could have taken the key and made a copy," she argued, still looking for a reason to explain what she knew to be true.

"I didn't say—"

"Elise!" After a quick rap on her front door, a deep, clipped voice bellowed from the foyer below.

With a woof, Spike sprang to his feet.

"George?" She swung her head toward the sound of the deputy commissioner calling her name through the rooms on the main floor.

"Ma'am, wait." Officer Hale put his arm out to block her rush toward the bedroom door, but Elise skirted around him. "We don't know who—"

"I do. G... Commissioner? What are you doing here?"

Spike hurried down the steps after her. The broad back of George Madigan's navy suit jacket turned to reveal an open collar and that inviting chest. At the last second, common sense reined in Elise's relief, and she stopped herself from running straight into his arms, denying herself the haven of security he offered.

But he clasped her shoulders anyway, his slightly rough hands making contact that shot through her skin like a bolt of lightning, exciting frayed nerves and weakening a resolve that couldn't handle many more demands on it. "I heard your address on the scanner driving home. I called Dispatch to verify that you'd reported an intruder. Officer Boyd just let me in." Although he lowered the volume of his voice, there was no less authority behind it. "Are you okay?"

Denton Hale loomed up like a shadow behind her on the stairs. "I didn't know you two were..." The tone of the officer's voice snapped to attention. "The scene is secure, sir."

Without asking permission or apologizing for startling her, George tucked Elise to his side, draping an arm around her shoulders to keep her snugged against his solid flank. "She works for me, Denton. That's all you need to know. But it doesn't matter who she is. Get outside with your partner, Boyd, and double-check that everything's secure, from the basement to the attic. Don't forget her car and the garage, too."

"Her car wasn't here when the alleged intruder—"

Elise snapped her gaze up. "Alleged?"

She felt a squeeze on her shoulder as George moved them out of the uniformed officer's path to the front door. "Do it. Canvas the neighborhood, too. Get statements from anyone who saw anything around Miss Brown's house today. Ask if there have been any other break-ins or suspicious activity in the area."

"Boyd is already doing that."

"Good. Then you'd better get out there and help him. There are a lot of homes on this street."

"Yes, sir." Denton pulled his cap from his rear pocket, squeezing it in his fist before turning to Elise. "Ma'am, if anything I said or did—"

"Now." George dismissed Hale before he finished his apology. As soon as the door closed behind the officer, George tugged Elise into step beside him and crossed through the arch into her shrouded living room. "So what did he say or do to upset you?"

"He took my statement."

"And?"

Elise's feet didn't seem to be moving under their own power. "I don't think he believed me."

George may have muttered a curse. But whether it was aimed at Officer Hale or the cluttered state of her house, she couldn't tell. Other than a pause to orient himself to the drop cloths and sawhorses in front of the fireplace, George led her to the furniture that had all been stacked against the opposite wall. Even a small black dog sniffing around his feet didn't slow him down or alter the purpose of his stride. "Don't you generate any heat, woman? It's a hundred degrees out and you're freezing."

He shrugged out of his jacket and wrapped it around her. Elise shivered at the shock of his scent and lingering body heat sliding over her chilled skin.

"There was a man in my house." She sounded like a worn-out recording.

"I know." George pulled the paint tarp off her sofa and tossed it to the floor. He unloaded the two end tables she'd stored on top of the cushions before he took her hand and urged her to sit.

"I think he let Spike get out the door when he came in. Or else he put him out on purpose." It was the only scenario that made sense. If any of this made sense. Elise clutched the suit jacket together over her dress, shaking at the knowledge of what could have happened to her if she'd met him face-to-face. "He was in my bedroom."

The cushion beside her sank and her balance shifted as George sat down. "I believe you."

"Even if there's no evidence?" Elise glanced up to see if he was simply trying to placate her the way Officer Hale had. "The doors were locked. And nothing's missing."

"You may have scared him off before he had a chance to take anything. And a barking dog changes a lot of intruders' minds." He pulled both her hands between his and gently rubbed them. "Besides, you're too cold for me to doubt you. That means you had a real shock. It happened."

George Madigan's matter-of-fact tone did more to make her feel safe than two armed police officers and a robotic sounding dispatcher had. His simple statement of faith in her sanity swept out the cobwebs of self-doubt and touched her bruised heart.

Curling her legs beneath her, Elise pushed herself up, looping her arms about George's neck, knocking him into the back of the couch. "Thank you."

"For what...?" After a momentary hesitation, his chest expanded with a deep breath, meeting hers. When he exhaled, there was no more gap between them. He folded his arms around her, flattening one hand against her spine to anchor her to his body. He pushed aside the jacket's collar and threaded his fingers into the short hair at her nape to massage the tension in her neck. "You're okay. You're safe now. No one's going to hurt you."

Elise turned her cheek into the soft rasp of his evening beard stubble, feeling the vibration of his deep voice against her ear. Her own fingertips brushed against the dark silk of his hair as she rode each measured breath on his chest, absorbing his heat. George was solid and real. There was no mistaking this vital, caring man for a figment of her imagination. "I almost wish they would."

"Hurt you? I'm going to disagree with that idea, if you don't mind."

"But all this is making me think I'm going crazy. There are too many things that I can't explain." He took the edge off her raw nerves with his calm voice and soothing massage. "I'm not crazy. I'm not."

"What do you mean by 'all this'?" His fingers stilled when she shook her head, reluctant to answer. He unwound her arms from his neck and let her slide down onto his lap. Pulling the jacket back over her shoulders, he urged her grasping hands to settle at the lapels. Once she was holding the coat together at her neck, George brushed the hair off her forehead and pressed his lips against the spot. "Talk to me."

It was the gentlest of kisses, and maybe the most dangerous. Because, while a lingering kiss to the forehead was soothing, patient, kind—the caress also gave her a glimpse of what George's lips might feel like against hers. They were firm. Masculine. Pure, incandescent heat. She had a feeling that a man of his experience might know exactly what to do with those lips, too.

Elise's breath locked in her chest at the desire suddenly humming between them. Her fingers slipped from the jacket to the starched crispness of his unbuttoned collar. "George?" she breathed.

"Beats sir." For a split second, his gray eyes locked on to hers. They were so close, she could read every hue of granite, smoke and steel in the irises there. Then his gaze dropped lower, to her mouth, and a deep-pitched groan rumbled beneath her hands.

George dipped his head, touching his mouth to hers, kindling a slow, liquid fire in Elise's blood that chased away the chill of doubt and fear. The kiss was as tender as the graze across her forehead had been. A simple meeting of skin against skin. At first.

When she didn't resist, George's lips urged hers apart. His warm breath rushed in to mingle with hers. Elise's fingers fisted in his shirt. Her tongue darted out to sample the smooth, male plane of his bottom lip, and his own tongue forced hers back to taste the soft skin inside her mouth. The cold she'd felt moments earlier shattered with bursts of heat inside her belly and at the tips of her breasts.

It was, by far, the most potent, most surprising, most spontaneous response she'd ever had to a man's kiss. Every place they touched—her lips, her earlobes and neck where he held her against his mouth, her fingers clinging to the muscles of his chest, her hip and bottom nestled against his thighs—was on fire.

And that's when the alarm bells went off inside her head and she knew she had to stop. She eased her grip on George's collar and pushed at his chin, leaning back when he moved to resume the kiss. "What are you doing?" she asked on a throaty whisper.

George's fingers tensed before he untangled them from her hair. "I'm more rusty at this than I thought if you have to ask."

She'd loved Quinn Gallagher with hopeless devotion. She'd given herself to Nikolai Titov out of loneliness and lust. But this was different. She'd never felt this alive, this desired, this needy in a man's arms before. And if anything frightened her, it was the knowledge that she could very easily fall for George Madigan—for the wrong man—all over again. "I...I can't. We can't."

"My mistake." His eyes shuttered as he moved his hands to her waist and lifted her off his lap. Elise landed on the seat cushion beside him, catching herself before she tumbled back into his side.

"No. I was a part of that as much as you were. I'm sorry. I wasn't thinking for a minute there. I was just...scared." She pointed to his grim expression, then to her own shaky smile. "Boss, assistant—remember?" He might think she was quoting departmental protocol, but reminding herself of the hazards of getting into a relationship with this man was more a matter of her own emotional survival. "I shouldn't have encouraged you—"

"What else has happened besides the intruder

and the mystery of the roses?" George's tone was as sharply articulate and impersonal as it had been hushed and indulgent moments earlier.

Although the worst of the spooky chill that had numbed her of self-sufficiency and common sense had dissipated inside George's embrace, Elise reluctantly shrugged his jacket off her shoulders. She folded it neatly in her lap to return to him, fearing it was too much of an imposition to reject his kiss, yet still ask for his comfort. "George. It's not you. It's—"

"What else has happened?" So they weren't going to talk about that kiss. Because this, whatever it was, didn't—couldn't—exist between them. She'd said as much to him this morning. George rolled up his sleeves, literally and figuratively transforming himself into work mode. He nodded at the dog sitting at his feet, staring at them as if he wanted the people to make room for him on the crowded couch. "So this is the guy on your desk at work. What's his name?"

"Spike."

"Is he friendly?" Elise nodded, holding out the suit coat to return to him.

Instead of accepting the jacket, George reached down with one hand to scoop up the miniature poodle mix and set him on her lap. Spike immediately curled up on George's jacket and made himself at home. Elise would have tried to protect the coat if George wasn't already scratching the spoiled dog around his ears and making an instant friend. She tried to ignore the warmth of George's hip and thigh butting against hers. She tried to make sense of the mature, no-nonsense cop wooing her closest ally. She tried to dismiss the confusing emotions warring inside her.

George was her boss, fourteen years her senior, a workaholic like herself. He carried weighty responsibilities on his shoulders. Responsibilities she'd sworn to support. Not the man she would have chosen to be so viscerally attracted to.

It was her talent to form relationships with the wrong men. And while she believed George was a good man, he wasn't the man for her and she would certainly get hurt again.

He was her friend. There were few people she trusted so implicitly. She didn't want to screw that up.

She needed him to ground her in the current, crazy chaos of her life with his decisive words and stalwart support.

She wanted him to kiss her again.

George caught her staring at him when he lifted his stony gaze to hers. Understandably, he misread her silence as a reluctance to share the details of the past few days. "If you won't talk to me, then tell Spike what's going on."

The man was dead serious. Elise dropped her gaze from those probing eyes and stroked the silky curls of Spike's hair. "I can't explain any of it."

"Yes, you can."

Boss. Friend. Security. George Madigan was all those things. It was enough.

And with nothing more than a relaxed little dog binding them together, Elise talked. She told George about the significance of twenty-three roses, how her affair with Nikolai Titov had lasted twenty-three days before he'd been deported to Lukinburg and was murdered. He already knew about Titov's vendetta against her former boss, Quinn Gallagher, but he listened patiently when she told him how she'd unwittingly given Titov and his hit squad access to information on GSS Security and Quinn's personal schedule. And though she'd never met Aleksandr Titov, the fact that Nikolai's brother had come to Kansas City was a little unsettling. She talked about the house key and how the police officers had found it in its box as if the thing had never gone missing at all. She talked about the dog greeting her in the front yard, and the crash and footsteps they'd heard upstairs. She reminded George that no one else had seen the key missing or heard the weird phone call in her office. No one could prove that the very same bouquet she'd taken to the hospital had been returned to her desk or she hadn't left Spike outside herself or that there had ever been an intruder in her home.

When she was done, Elise hugged the dog against her chest. "At least you're okay, sweetie. You could have been hit by a car, running loose like that. Or gotten heatstroke."

George moved to the edge of the couch, turning to face her. "Someone's trying to scare you."

"They're succeeding."

"Any idea why? Could someone be trying to discredit you for some reason? Got any old boyfriends you've ticked off?"

She shook her head. "That's the scariest part—I have no idea why these things are happening to me. I mean, what's the point?"

George pushed to his feet. "You haven't been yourself the past couple of days. If nothing else, these mind games have disrupted the efficiency of my office."

Elise cradled Spike in her arms and stood. "I'm sorry."

"I'm not worried about you doing your job.

Even on your worst day you get more done than any assistant I've had." He picked his suit jacket up off the floor and shook it open. "I'm throwing out a possible motive. Budget shortfalls and increased demand for trained personnel don't make me a popular man."

"I would never let anything happen that could impact KCPD or the deputy commissioner's office." She wouldn't betray the people she worked with ever again. "After what happened with Quinn Gallagher, I keep my job and my private life separate."

"You and Quinn?" He paused in the middle of buttoning his shirt cuff. His gray eyes zeroed in on her. She hadn't confessed to unrequited love and heartbreak. But maybe George was reading between the lines of the story she'd told. "That explains a lot."

Maybe it was all the explanation he needed to dismiss that kiss. Maybe she should dismiss it, too. But he'd seemed so...insulted that she had.

"George. I truly am...attracted to you, and I value our friendship. But there are a lot of reasons why we can't—"

But Elise never got to finish. Her front door opened and James Westbrook stormed in. "Lise? Baby, what happened? Are you okay?"

He brushed off the police officer who tried to stop him. "Let go of me."

Denton Hale caught James firmly by the arm this time and pulled him back into the archway. "I'm sorry, sir. Since you were here, I didn't think to relock the door. I saw him from across the street and tried to stop him before he got in. He says he's a friend of Miss Brown's."

James jerked his arm free and took a step closer. "I am a friend. Lise, tell them."

George took his time shrugging into his jacket and adjusting his cuffs, planting himself in the middle of the room's narrow pathway. James would have to climb over paint cans and sawhorses if he wanted to get any closer to her. "Is Miss Brown expecting you?" he asked.

"No," Elise answered. "Why are you here?"

"Lise!" James's gaze darted from Elise to George and back to her. With a noisy sigh, he stayed where he was and held up a bundle of letters and ad flyers. "Your mailbox was open out front. So I brought it in for you. What's with all the cops?"

"Answer her question," George insisted.

Concern morphed into anger in James's expression. "I'm not talking to you."

"Answer...the question."

"I knew you were upset last night so I came

over to take you to dinner and apologize. As friends." James negated the sincerity of his apology by glaring through his glasses at her around the jut of George's shoulder. "Who is this guy? Is he why you've been avoiding me?"

Elise touched George's arm to nudge him over a step so she could stand beside him. When her fingers lingered against the summer-weight wool of his sleeve, James's gaze landed on the spot and she quickly pulled away. "Someone broke in, but nothing was taken and I'm not hurt. This is the man I work for at KCPD, George Madigan. Deputy Commissioner, this is James Westbrook."

James seemed to calm down as if the hot air of his temper was a balloon that had suddenly popped. "Oh. Your boss. Good to meet you."

Although George shook the hand James offered, he was already backing James toward the foyer. "I'll walk you out."

But when they reached the door, James splayed his fingers at the waist of his pressed jeans and held his ground. "Is there some reason why I can't stay? We can order a pizza. We don't have to go out."

Elise followed the three men into the foyer. "I'm really tired, James. I'd be lousy company."

There was a momentary glitch in the diplomatic charm of his blue eyes. "I'll take a rain check, then." He handed Elise her mail, palmed Spike's head and leaned in to kiss her cheek. "Be sure you lock your doors. I wouldn't want anything to happen to you. Call you tomorrow?"

Whatever. She had no energy left to say even a polite no. "Good night, James."

With an order to Officer Hale to escort the unwanted guest back to his car, George pushed the door shut, leaning against it and crossing his arms. "He's the guy I alibied you out for, isn't he."

There was no avoiding that probing gaze. "We used to date. Years ago. We went our separate ways by mutual agreement."

"Does he know that? That you're not interested?"

"He's lived overseas for several years. Now that he's back in Kansas City, he doesn't know that many people. He's just looking for companionship." George's eyes never wavered, never blinked. Elise bristled with a shot of defensive anger. "You don't think James is behind this craziness, do you? He's more likely to pester me into saying yes to him than he is to terrorize me."

Those broad shoulders lifted with a shrug. "I've dealt with crazier scenarios. Maybe he thought you'd get scared enough that you'd turn to him for comfort."

"James doesn't make me feel safe. You…"

The moment of anger passed on a noiseless sigh and Elise dropped her gaze to the middle of his chest. She'd already shared way too much of her personal life for the impersonal relationship she claimed to want.

"I do." George straightened away from the door, nodding as if she'd spoken the words out loud. "Okay. Then here's what we do. Call someone to change this lock first thing in the morning. I'll post a black-and-white unit outside tonight."

"The city can't afford to dedicate a unit just for me. You don't have to do that."

"Yes, I do. It's my job to allocate funds and personnel where they're needed most. They're needed here tonight." She recognized that tone, the one that said *I'm in charge and what I say goes.*

"No." Whether she was really thinking about the common good or if she was distancing herself from the temptation of letting this powerful man take care of her, of letting him become even more involved in her life, she wasn't sure. But she protested, anyway. "Think of the resentment. Officers like Denton Hale are already worried about their next paycheck. With the increased power demands, the city is struggling to make ends meet. You can't just order someone to babysit me because a few weird things have happened. The police have more important jobs to do right now."

"A trespasser in your house is a real crime, Elise."

"But attacks on utility workers are more important."

"You're important." With her arms full of dog and mail, he reached out to brush aside a loose wave of hair that had fallen over her cheek. "All right. I'll work something else out. But I need you to be safe, Elise. You're too valuable to me."

As his assistant. As the fuel that made his office run so successfully. It was a lovely compliment. Yet oddly disappointing. Still, Elise summoned a smile for him. "I'll see you tomorrow at work."

His fingertips lingered behind the shell of her ear, and for a moment she thought he might do something sweetly reassuring like kiss her on the forehead again. Instead, he scratched the dog's head one more time. "Keep an eye on her, Spike."

When the dog nuzzled his hand, the man almost smiled. But that wasn't George Madigan's way. He opened the door and listed off directions just like he did at the office every morning. "Bring that spare key into the house and lock this when I leave. Call me or 9-1-1 if you see or hear anything else that's suspicious. If something seems off to you, it probably is."

"Yes, sir."

He arched a dark eyebrow. "Not funny."

Elise smiled. Because it was her way. And while they couldn't admit to this attraction or discuss that kiss, she was grateful that he'd been here for her this evening. "Thank you for everything. I'll be careful. Good night, George."

"Good night, Elise."

She watched him stride down the porch steps to his silver Suburban, stopping to have a word with Denton Hale and his partner. George looked up and down the street, probably verifying, like her, that James had driven away. When he looked back at her, Elise set Spike down on the floor. She pulled the key box from the flowerpot and went back inside to lock both the knob and dead bolt.

Then she turned on the porch light, letting George know she was following his instructions and was secure inside. She watched at the front window until Hale and his partner left in their police cruiser and George climbed inside his SUV.

Feeling drained from tip to toe, Elise kicked off her shoes and carried the mail to the kitchen. The light in the foyer flickered when she cranked up the air conditioner to cool the first floor. After shutting off the extra interior lights to conserve electricity, she set the end tables back on the sofa and covered them all with the paint tarp, erasing the reminder of being held in George's arms.

She could do this. She had Spike for company. She didn't need a man in her life, certainly not George Madigan with his surprising tenderness and chivalrous protective streak. Tomorrow would be a normal day. Maybe she'd even get lucky and the temperatures would break and the city would get some much needed rain.

A girl could dream, couldn't she?

Too tired to fix a meal, Elise nonetheless wound up in the kitchen. She couldn't take anything for her headache unless she had food in her stomach, and if she didn't eat, the throbbing would only get worse. So she tossed Spike a rawhide chew to nibble on while she grabbed a yogurt cup and half of a chocolate bar from the fridge. With only the light from the range hood to illuminate the shadows, she sat down on a stool at the island's granite countertop to force a few bites down her throat and sort through mail. A couple of bills, summer sale notices from local merchants, a postcard from her parents vacationing in Glacier National Park and one envelope that had neither a return address nor a familiar business logo. She slit open the envelope and pulled out the letter.

Elise's spoon clattered onto the countertop. Suddenly, the air-conditioning was working very, very well.

I hate it when you make me angry, Elise. I wasn't pleased to see you give away my roses. That's why I brought them back. When I give you a gift, I need you to treasure it the way I treasure you. I forgive you this time, but don't make that mistake again.
I Love You.

"Who...?" she whispered, tossing aside the letter. The stool toppled over when she hopped off and backed away from the disturbing message. Elise barely heard Spike's startled yelp through the haze of fear and madness clouding her brain. When her back hit the wall behind her, she cried out as if an unknown hand had touched her shoulder.

But the start was enough to clear one thought in her head.

"George." *Call me. I need you to be safe.*

Screw practicality and relationships that shouldn't be.

Elise dumped her purse onto the counter, digging out her phone and racing from the kitchen to put as much distance as she could between herself and that anonymous letter. Searching through the numbers as she and Spike climbed the stairs, she touched George Madigan's name and put the phone to her ear.

She dashed straight into her bedroom and opened the top drawer of her dresser to pull out a pair of socks. Her home should feel like a sanctuary, not a padded cell. She intended to put on her running shoes, hook Spike to his leash and go out into the steamy night air because even the suffocating humidity was preferable to the hazards sneaking their way inside her home.

George's number rang once.

Elise pushed the lingerie around in her drawer. Her socks were always on the left-hand side. Her cash-filled envelope of fun money was still stashed beneath them. "What...?" She was imagining the subtle shift in things.

She shoved the drawer shut as the phone rang a third time and she opened the second drawer. Elise rifled through the contents there before opening the next two. This wasn't right. Why wasn't this right? She glanced over at the empty laundry basket by her closet. Everything had been neatly folded and put away. Everything.

"Oh, God." She pressed her fist to her mouth to keep from retching. Then she pulled open the top drawer again and tossed everything onto the bed. *One. Two. Three. Four.*

She'd counted to five when the phone stopped ringing. "George!"

"What's wrong?"

"I need you." Forgetting her socks and shoes, she staggered back to the landing and sat on the top step, hugging her knees to her chest, turning her head at every creak and groan of the big empty house. Something slammed in the distance, jerking her in her seat. "Please come back."

His clipped voice was deep, urgent. "Is someone there?"

"I don't know what's happening to me—" She screamed at the loud pounding on her front door.

Spike dashed past her, barking at the commotion at the front of the house. The bell rang, over and over. "Open the damn door!"

"George?"

"Hang up the phone and open—"

Elise was already running down the stairs. "How did you get here so fast?"

She left her phone on the newel post and attacked the locks. She could hear George shouting through the front window now. "I was parked out front. I volunteered for guard duty tonight." She flung open the door and he marched inside. "What's going on?"

"I don't know." Elise walked straight into his chest. Circling her arms beneath his jacket, she burrowed her cheek into his shoulder and held on tight to his familiar, welcome strength. His chin settled at the crown of her hair and his arms folded around her, pulling her snug against his hardness and heat, absorbing every shaking molecule of her body.

"I was on the phone, recruiting some backup to help keep an eye on things, or I would have answered your call sooner."

"Just shut up and hold me."

"I am holding you." His fingers tunneled into her hair. The buttons of his shirt crushed into her skin beneath her dress. And still, she snuggled closer. "Honey, you need to talk to me."

"In the kitchen." She felt his body shift and she curled her fingers into the back of his shirt, keeping him with her. "He sent me a letter. He said he loves me."

"Who?"

"I don't know." She sniffed back a silent sob. "That's not all. When he was in my bedroom... there is something missing. Nothing significant. I didn't even notice it at first."

A curse grumbled through his chest. "Tell me."

Elise felt so chilled and dizzy, she didn't think she'd still be standing if George's arms weren't around her.

"He stole a pair of my panties."

Chapter Five

"I'm not asking you to do this."

The tremulous pulse along Elise's pale jaw-line sent George a different message. This gas lighting campaign was taking a toll on her. "You think this is going to go away on its own?"

She'd had sixteen messages on her answering machine by the time she got around to listening to it last night. All untraceable, all saying the same thing in a breathy, toneless, increasingly drunk or distressed voice. "I love you." Sixteen times. Sixteen counts of harassment at the very least.

No, this wasn't going away on its own.

"But to get other people involved when we're already blurring the lines between work and—"

"It's not up for debate, Elise. Something needs to be done."

Unsure whether those tired eyes were flashing anger, fear or annoyance at his peremptory end to her subtle warning reminders, George braced his fists on the sill of his office window and looked up into the clear blue sky. Not even ten in the morning and the sun was already cooking the city.

But as this blast of summer neared its breaking point, Mother Nature was already showing signs of her temper with some pretty violent weather. From Oklahoma up the state line into northeast Missouri, they'd already had three tornado watches in the past two weeks. Torrential rains out west had caused flash flooding and runoff that was filling up rivers and streams that had been dry arroyos through years of drought, and now all that extra water and debris was flowing into the Missouri River. The Missouri, in turn, cut through the middle of K.C., bringing humidity to the city, drawing nightly lightning storms like a magnet, taunting them with the promise of rain that dried up before it ever reached the parched earth. Something bad was brewing in the heart of the Midwest. It was going to hit them hard.

And George had a feeling that Kansas City was going to be smack-dab in the middle of whatever was coming. Despite the stress of the past few weeks, he trusted that KCPD, other first responders and the citizens of K.C. themselves, would rise to the occasion to get through the coming crisis.

A storm was already brewing in his executive assistant's life. And whatever Elise Brown had to deal with, he was dealing with it, too. She was his right hand, the smiling face who greeted him every morning, the patience and caring that tempered his worst days and made the high-pressure issues he had to deal with seem practically routine. And because he needed her, he needed to do this for her.

Protect the city. Protect the department. Protect the office. Protect her.

George glanced over at the brunette waiting dutifully beside his desk and wished to hell he could do even more to ease the tension that kept her smile flatlined and her posture ramrod straight this morning. "Put the call on speakerphone. We all need to hear this. If you think it'll be too much for you, you don't have to stay."

"I'm staying." With a quick breath that sounded as if she was gearing up for battle, Elise punched the flashing button on his phone and placed the receiver in its cradle to make the conference call happen. "Dr. Kilpatrick? Elise Brown here again. I have the deputy commissioner here, as well as Detective Nick Fensom and his wife, CSI Annie Fensom."

George turned back to the room, nodding his thanks to his nephew and niece-in-law for answering his early morning call for a little off-the-record help. The woman on the phone was a friend who worked as a departmental psychologist and criminal profiler for KCPD. "I'm here, Elise. Good morning, George. And I know Nick and Annie well. We worked together on the Rose Red Rapist task force."

Nick looked like the detective George had once been, with his badge hanging around his neck over his black T-shirt and his sidearm holstered to the belt of his jeans. "Mornin', Dr. Kate." He reached across the space between the two guest chairs and batted at one of his wife's dark brown curls, pulling her attention from the taunting love letter she'd been studying. "Annie says 'hi,' too."

"Engrossed in some piece of evidence, I imagine," Kate teased.

Annie's cheeks dotted with embarrassment before she returned the paper and envelope back to the plastic bag George had sealed it in and peeled off her examination gloves. "Yes, ma'am. Good morning."

George's chest expanded with an impatient sigh. *Enough pleasantries.* "Kate, did you get a chance to read a copy of the note I had Elise fax you this morning?"

"I did." Understanding the urgency of the situation surrounding Elise, the police psychologist got down to the business of offering the professional evaluation George had asked for. "One anonymous letter isn't much to go on. But with the gifts and break-in that you mentioned, and the fact that he took a souvenir, it's creating a disturbing pattern. I can give you a general idea of the type of man who may be behind it."

Kate Kilpatrick's clinical description of recent events seemed to hit Elise like a blow to the midsection. As she hugged her waist, George rolled his chair around the desk to her. When the stubborn thing wouldn't sit immediately, George touched her elbow. Damn. The stalwart facade and show of independence were costing her. But as soon as he rubbed his hand up her arm to instill some warmth into her chilled skin, she pulled away from even that impersonal contact and sat.

"I didn't realize there was more than one kind of stalker." Elise picked up her laptop from the desk and set it on her lap, opening a file to take notes or doodle or busy herself with whatever it was she suddenly needed to do besides interact with him.

"Yes, there is," Kate replied, probably unaware of the tension on this end of the call.

But Nick's raised eyebrow and glance toward Elise told George that his nephew seemed to think there might be something more prompting this meeting than protecting one of the department's professional assets.

Ignoring his nephew's curious perusal, George folded his arms across his chest and sat on the front edge of his desk. "So what did the note tell you about this guy, Kate?"

"The *I*'s the sender uses in every sentence could indicate an egocentric dysfunction," the psychologist said. "That means the sender lacks an objective perspective of the world around him."

"Explain," George said.

"He probably functions reasonably well in society—he can hold a job and have relationships. But he projects his feelings and values onto others, and assumes they think and feel the same way."

"Sounds pretty arrogant," Nick commented.

"Most psychopaths typically are."

"Psychopath?" Elise murmured. Her fingers stilled over her laptop keys. "How would I attract a psychopath?"

George curled his hands into fists, quelling

the urge to push past the distance and decorum Elise had insisted upon in the light of day, and go to her. "Bottom line, Kate. Is a perp who fits this profile dangerous?"

Her lengthy pause wasn't terribly reassuring. "He may see disagreement as a personal insult—even as an attack. And that could make him angry."

Nick grunted a curse that matched his own. "Let me guess, he takes that anger out on the target of his affection?"

"It's possible," Dr. Kilpatrick agreed. "With a lesser degree of dysfunction, he'd probably simply turn his attention to someone else who feeds his ego. But if this guy has become obsessed with a particular target, then yes, he could definitely be a threat if he feels she's disrespecting him or cheating on him."

"Cheating?" Elise's voice was stronger.

"Yes. Take a married woman, for example, if he was fixated on her, then he'd see her normal relationship with her husband as cheating. He'd want to punish her for that perceived betrayal."

"Oh, my God."

Exactly what he'd been afraid of. George pushed away from his desk. He was good enough at pulling the right people together to get a job done, but physically protecting Elise would require a different strategy. "Thanks, Kate. I appreciate the input."

"Before you hang up…" George paused with his hand over the phone. He'd been ready to do just that. "Elise is your assistant, isn't she?"

George stuffed his hand into the pocket of his tan slacks. "She is."

"Not to throw a wrench into your fact-finding meeting, but have you considered the possibility that your perp may be a copycat? This is pretty textbook stuff thus far—I've discussed this same unsub profile in classes I've taught at the university. Heck, you can read it online if you know what to look for." Dr. Kilpatrick was as thorough at her job as he'd hired her to be. "Think about your office, George. This perp could be targeting Elise as a means to get to you."

Elise's gaze shot up to his. "I would never—"

"I've considered it." George silenced the protest Elise had made more than once the night before. Whatever her ex-boyfriend Nikolai Titov had done to screw with her head to gain access to Gallagher Security Systems info, the damage he'd done to Elise's self-assurance was unforgivable. He didn't doubt her loyalty to him or KCPD for one moment. But the thought that Elise believed she was so weak willed that she'd betray him or the sensitive information in this office bothered him more than the fear of an unknown stalker that raised goose bumps along her soft skin. "We're still in the process of gathering facts to see if we need to launch an investigation. Thanks, Kate."

"Anytime. Stay safe, Miss Brown. Goodbye, everyone."

With Elise's distracted focus turned down to the screen of her laptop, George reached across the desk to disconnect the call himself.

The shadows under her pretty blue eyes indicated the restless sleep she'd had. Even though George had spent the night on the couch in the construction zone of her living room to offer some degree of security, and she'd had that pint-size guard dog upstairs to keep her company, Elise's bed had rattled overhead as she'd tossed and turned. And when she couldn't fight her troubled thoughts any longer, she'd gotten up and turned on lights and spent an hour or more opening closets and drawers and moving things around in muffled noises that sounded suspiciously like cleaning house…or taking inventory to make sure nothing else had been touched or taken by the intruder.

Fueled by the aching frustration in his gut, George had lain awake most of the night, too, deciding exactly what he should do to help. Elise's problem wasn't something he could fix by writing a report, negotiating a compromise or issuing a statement.

This was old-school. She needed someone to stand between her and the nut job who was stalking her. She needed a man in her life. A bodyguard. She needed a cop.

More than anything—more than he should—George wanted to be that man.

But his years behind a desk had made him soft. Sure, he passed all his physicals and kept in shape, but when was the last time he'd run after a perp and taken him down? He'd grown more cerebral, less instinctive. The sidearm he'd strapped onto his belt this morning felt heavy against his hip. He hadn't taken the lead on an investigation since he'd left the Narcotics division. He was used to giving the orders, letting his team make things happen while he watched the budget, supplied the equipment and approved the manpower they needed to do their job.

Elise's intelligence, caring patience and endless legs gave a man plenty to notice and appreciate. But there was something more than the dark caramel hair and undeniable efficiency that had gotten beneath his hardened exterior.

For years he hadn't cared about anyone on this gut-deep level. He loved his sister and her family. He cared about Courtney being happy. But he hadn't wanted anything like this for himself for a long time. There was a vulnerability about Elise Brown that had awakened some basic primal need in him. He hadn't even thought about falling in love again, about being with a woman for something more than companionship. But Elise had him thinking.

That forbidden kiss.

Those tight embraces.

I need you.

What was he supposed to make of a woman who called him with a panicked request like that and clung to him like a second skin, yet pushed him away and quoted departmental protocol if he overstepped the lines of friendly concern or, God forbid, tried to get ahead of the slimy psychopath who'd made her so afraid?

George's chest expanded with a deep breath. Being a frontline cop wasn't the only skill that had gone rusty on him. Elise's fingers were moving over her keyboard again, and she seemed completely oblivious to his assessing gaze and uncharacteristic introspection.

"Uncle George?" Startled from his thoughts by his nephew's voice, George reached up to massage the tension beneath his collar before slowly turning, masking any reaction. Nick had pulled out his notebook and pen, ready to work. And if that was suspicion narrowing the blue eyes that looked so like his sister's, it had better be aimed at finding answers for Elise, not reading anything into George's long silence. "I said, do we have any suspects?"

Propping his hip on the edge of his desk, George turned his attention to the family he'd called in for help with this unsanctioned investigation. "Here's the plan. Annie, I need you to do your scientific magic and find out who sent that letter."

"I can swab the seal and stamp for any DNA trace, but I won't make any guarantees. If he's not in the system, I'd need more evidence to confirm a match. And this guy seems to be making a concerted effort to remain anonymous." Annie carefully placed the sealed evidence inside her kit and locked it. Her explanation included Elise, drawing her back into the conversation. "I didn't find any prints in your bedroom or on that vase except for your own. Even if there are prints on this letter, we'll have nothing to compare them to, making it difficult to even know if it's the same guy."

"It has to be," Elise said.

"He's smart," George conceded. "I wouldn't be surprised if he's wearing gloves."

"Anyone wearing gloves would stand out in this heat, wouldn't they?" Elise suggested. "We could look for that."

"If we get a visual on him, yes. But I'm hoping we can ID this guy before he ever gets that close to you." George turned to his nephew. "Nick. Compile a list of all the men in Elise's life—everyone from family friends to men she's dated to casual acquaintances."

"I'm already working on it," Elise said, turning her laptop around to show them a screenful of names. "I started with my dad and worked my way down to the kid who bags my groceries at the store. I put asterisks next to a couple I thought might hold some kind of grudge against me—"

"Like Westbrook?" George asked. Preppy-boy with the glasses had acted as if he had some sort of proprietary claim on Elise last night, which put him at the top of George's suspect list. Of course, he'd still been mentally stomping out the residual embers from that incendiary kiss he and Elise had shared when Westbrook had stormed in, so he was pretty sure his objectivity had been in question. "Anyone else?"

Elise shrugged. "I can't imagine that James

would want to hurt me, and I don't know anyone that I've insulted or angered like Dr. Kilpatrick suggested, certainly not intentionally. In a lot of ways, I live a pretty unremarkable life. And what if it's someone I haven't thought of, or don't even know?"

Nick pointed to her computer. "I'll give you my number. If you send me that list, it'll give me a place to start running background checks, at least."

Nodding, Elise set to work organizing the list and attaching it to an email. But a second later, she raised her head. "What about Alexsandr Titov?"

"Who's that?" Nick asked.

George could guess what she was thinking. "He's the brother of that European mobster who went after Quinn Gallagher and GSS a few years back—blamed Quinn for his son's death. Elise worked at GSS during that time."

Nick whistled between his teeth. "You were caught up in that mess?"

George interrupted before Elise could answer or confess to the collusion she blamed herself for. "Quinn's on his way over here to discuss his suspicions about why Alexsandr is in Kansas City."

"His timing is a little hinky, considering

what's going on with Miss Brown. Is he connected to a foreign mob, too?" Nick shook his head and jotted a note when George didn't answer. "I'll find out."

But Elise refused to avoid the subject George had tried to protect her from. "It's the same thing his brother, Nikolai, did to me when I worked for GSS." She set her laptop on the desk and stood, clearly agitated by her thoughts. "Oh, not the threatening love letter and creepy stuff. But, seeing me as the weak link and preying on that."

"The weak link to what?" Annie looked from George to Elise as they faced off. "Are you talking about what Dr. Kate said? If our unsub is a copycat instead of some pervert psychopath?"

Elise tilted her eyes up to George. "I would never betray you or this office. I would never jeopardize the work KCPD is doing or reveal any kind of sensitive information."

"I know you wouldn't."

"I did it before."

"No." Forgetting their audience, George took her by the shoulders, holding on tighter and dipping his face closer to hers when she would have twisted away. "You didn't. Nikolai Titov was a selfish bastard who took advantage of you when you were hurting. He used you."

"I'm hurting now, George. I'm frightened, and I don't know how to make it stop." Her hands settled at his biceps, ready to push him away, but somehow curling into the cotton of his sleeves instead. "What if I make the same mistake again? I wouldn't mean to, but I could. It may not be Mr. Titov. It could be someone else who wants something. The budget negotiations are going to determine who gets to keep his job and who's going on probation. Aren't there plenty of officers who'd like to have the inside scoop on that? The city's on edge with this heat wave—what if someone wants to take advantage of the emergency response procedures we have in place to rob a bank or commit some other crime when your officers are focused elsewhere? I have access to that information, just like you do."

"Elise, I trust you."

"Maybe you shouldn't."

"Elise—"

"It's nearly ten o'clock." She smoothed the wrinkles she'd made in his shirt—one stroke, two—before snatching her fingers away and quickly picking up her laptop. "I'd better go out to my office to meet Quinn for his appointment. He's usually very prompt."

"Ma'am." Nick stood when she headed for the door. "We'll get this guy."

Elise paused with her hand on the doorknob and looked over her shoulder to Nick and Annie. Her smile might not have reached her eyes, but it was there. "Thank you for your help."

Then she was gone and the barrier of an office door had been resurrected between them. George couldn't help but notice he hadn't been included in that thank-you. Maybe he was the one who should be worried about his sanity if he was still thinking there could be something more than a professional relationship between them.

"She's wound up pretty tight," Nick said, tucking his notebook into his back pocket. "Do you think this stalker is going to hurt her?" George's brooding silence was answer enough. With a nod, Nick bent down to pick up Annie's investigation kit. "We'll get to work."

"Sorry to chase you kids out, but I've got a meeting." His eyes were burning by the time he blinked and tore his gaze from the door to shake his nephew's hand. "I'll hear from you later?"

"I'll make it priority one today."

"Same here." Annie stretched up on her tiptoes to give George a hug. "I'll call with whatever results I get from the lab."

He hugged the petite woman right back. "Thanks. I know I'm asking a lot of you both to volunteer your time to help the old man. I don't need to remind you that until we find more concrete evidence, this isn't an official investigation."

Nick shrugged off the apology. "You're family. You're the reason I became a cop. It's what the Madigans and Fensoms do...old man."

Annie swatted Nick's arm and scooted him toward the door. "You're not old, Uncle George. And Elise is very pretty. Her pupils dilated when you two argued. I think she likes you, too."

"We're just friends."

Nick grinned. "Don't tell me you didn't notice those legs going all the way up to her neck."

"Nicolas," George warned.

"Nick!"

Nick threw his arms out in protest, smiling down at Annie. "What? You get to tease him about the looks he's been giving her, but I don't?"

Annie pointed. "You open that door right now. We've got work to do."

"All right, all right. I get it. Their relationship is as unofficial as the investigation."

"There is no relationship."

"Uh-huh." Nick flipped George a salute and

opened the door. "Getting to work now. I'll have something to report by the end of the day."

The young couple left George's office, bickering back and forth in heated whispers, but holding hands and bumping shoulders together like the newlyweds they were as they exited into the hallway.

Well, hell. No wonder Elise was so adamant about keeping their own relationship professional and platonic. He'd already crossed some invisible barrier if Nick and Annie could spot the tension radiating between them after spending barely thirty minutes together. George planted his hands on his waist and stood in the middle of his office, willing the rawness inside him to go away.

As the line between boss and man blurred, George admitted that he wanted Elise with a fury he hadn't felt for any woman since long before he and Courtney had started to splinter. He liked holding her, feeling her sleek curves and soft skin pressed against him. He loved how her fingers snuck past that careful reserve of hers and latched on to him with a surprising passion. He wanted to kiss her again. Hell, he wanted to strip off those sensible dresses and kiss a lot more than that sweet mouth. He'd felt more alive, more like the man he used to be these past few days than he'd felt in years.

But he needed her to feel safe and confident and sure of her world again.

Elise would be the one risking her career if they got involved. If the board of review demoted or fired her for breaking KCPD protocol, she could claim sexual harassment and sue the department. Not that he thought Elise would be so vindictive and lie about an affair, but he didn't want her to go through a hassle like that. She didn't deserve it. Especially, with the nightmare she'd gone through with her previous job.

"Suck it up, Madigan." He had to keep it square in his head that Elise only needed his help, not his heart.

He could live without a special woman in his life—he'd done it well enough since his divorce. But he couldn't live with himself if anything happened to Elise Brown—at a stalker's hand or because of his own selfish desires. He needed to rope in his libido, get a grip on these burgeoning emotions and be what Elise needed him to be. A cop with considerable influence. Her protector. Nothing more. And certainly nothing less.

With his resolve firmly in place, George straightened the knot of his tie and strode out to Elise's office where he could hear friendly voices greeting one another.

Some resolve. He walked out to find Quinn Gallagher, invention genius and wealthy entrepreneur, lifting Elise onto her toes in a tight hug. Yep, that was definitely a stab of jealousy that hit him in the gut when her feet touched the carpet again and Elise beamed the big smile she'd denied George all morning.

George and Quinn were good friends who'd done a lot of business dealings together to benefit the department and Kansas City. Quinn was a happily married man—George had attended the wedding and even wished him well. But yeah, he wished that hug and smile had been for him.

Understanding the departmental rule forbidding romantic entanglements between police officers and their direct subordinates far better than he'd like, George crossed Elise's office with his hand outstretched to greet his friend. "Quinn. I was looking for another crisis to add to my list today. So what's raised a red flag about Alexsandr Titov coming to town?"

SETTING THE BLACK steel gun down on the counter beside the empty magazine that had housed fifteen bullets, George removed his noise-dampening headphones and pushed the button to bring up the paper target at KCPD's indoor firing range. The attendant had already gone home, and with C shift out on patrol or working at their desks in their respective precinct buildings, George was alone in the building's basement.

Good thing, too. He grunted a curse as the paper outline of a full-grown man flapped to a stop. He was all over the place with his shooting. He'd clipped an ear, hit three belly shots and landed the rest of his bullets on the picture's extremities—nice, if all he wanted to do was give a perp an interesting scar. He counted fifteen holes. At least all his shots had hit the paper. The eye doctor had promised him reading glasses in the near future, but the more likely culprit for his sad performance was simply a lack of being out in the field and practicing his skill as often as he once had.

"You used to be better than this, Madigan," he grumbled.

He sent the target back and reloaded the Glock's magazine. He used to have better hunches about suspects, too. But he was no closer to knowing who was terrorizing Elise than he'd been this morning. Quinn Gallagher had given him an interesting theory about

Alexsandr Titov. Although the Lukinburg native had no known ties to organized crime in his country, neither had his brother, Nikolai, until Quinn had closed the ammunition production factory Nikolai had run for him. Arms smugglers who'd used the factory's shipments to transport their contraband around the world had kidnapped and killed Nikolai's son in an effort to coerce him into reopening the plant. Nikolai had come to the U.S. supposedly to urge Quinn to reopen the plant, when in reality, he'd come to take revenge on the man he blamed for his son's death.

Was Alexsandr really in Kansas City to rebuild a business empire and restore his family's good name? Or was he, like Nikolai before him, here to avenge his family? Quinn had arranged a lunch meeting with Titov tomorrow, ostensibly to hear his pitch for working with GSS again and selling the goods produced in his newly opened factory to KCPD. But George and Quinn both were hoping to come away with a more accurate reading about Alexsandr, and whether or not he held a grudge against Quinn, his wife or Elise.

If Titov was legit, then that left a whole city full of potential nut jobs, resentful employees and desperate crooks who might be targeting Elise.

Yeah, he was doing a real whiz-bang job of keeping her safe.

George loaded the magazine into his gun and slipped the first bullet into the firing chamber. He was ready to put his headphones back on and yell, "Firing fifteen," when he heard the footsteps on the floor behind him.

"Target practice?" Some of the tension eased from George's shoulders as his nephew, Nick Fensom, strolled into the firing booth beside him. "I noticed you were carrying this morning. Haven't seen that for a while."

George set his gun on the counter, with the barrel facing away from them both. "Since the department is short staffed right now, I'm heading over to Elise's to park out front and keep an eye on her house tonight. Figured I'd better be armed with more than a big cup of coffee if I was going to do her any good. Didn't want to push my luck on recruiting more volunteers."

"Uh-huh."

He eyed the deceptive nonchalance in Nick's muscular frame as Nick leaned an elbow on the counter and peered downrange to assess George's lousy performance. "Do you have a report for me?"

"How is this thing with Elise Brown not personal for you?"

George groaned. Nick must have inherited his smart mouth from his brother-in-law's side of the family. "Let it go, Nick. She's closer to your age than she is to mine."

"So? She's an adult, isn't she?"

"She's understandably rattled by this anonymous maniac who thinks he's in love with her. Or who's pretending to be, at least." He propped his hands at his waist, shrugging off his nephew's fishing expedition. "If she's got this paternal thing going where I can use my experience and influence to make her feel safe, then that's what I'll do for her."

"That is the biggest crock of—"

"What did you find out today?" There. George's paternal tone was sharp enough to get Nick to straighten and pull his notebook from his back pocket. But he was still grinning.

"Well, her dad's clean. He's vacationing in Montana as we speak." He waved off George's pointed look and got serious. "Nobody else on the list she gave me popped up as an obvious suspect. No mental illness, no major crimes. Nobody on the special victims unit's watch list."

"What about Westbrook?"

Nick flipped a page in his notebook and scanned the information. "He moved to Korea right out of college. Climbed the corporate ladder pretty quickly. Last job was VP of finance with an international firm of lawyers in the Czech Republic. He's got money in the bank, rents an apartment downtown and bought two season tickets to the Chiefs this fall, so he's planning on staying around for a while."

George tugged at his rolled-up sleeves and folded his arms over his chest. "Any clue why he came back to the States?"

"The translator's English wasn't that good, and I know zero Czech, but I got the idea a romance soured on him. It sounds like the woman might have died. I could make out the word *accident* but not the details."

Since Westbrook shared history with Elise, George supposed it made sense for the man to try to rekindle whatever he'd once had with her. He didn't like that Westbrook wanted Elise to be a solace for his grief, but it made sense. The emotional upheaval could even explain his short temper. "I may talk to Kate Kilpatrick again tomorrow. I wonder if it's plausible for a man to fixate on another woman as a means of coping with a traumatic loss."

Nick slipped the notebook back into his pocket. "I didn't know K.C. was the place where middle-aged hearts came to heal."

Not this again. "Are you referring to me?"

Nick shrugged. "I don't need to be as smart as Annie and notice dilated pupils to see you've got a thing for Elise. It's the first time I've ever seen you this involved with a woman since Aunt Courtney."

Involved. He supposed there was no resolute will or ignoring of facts that could make this thing go away. George raked his fingers through his hair and released a weary breath. "I kissed her."

"Aunt Court?"

"Elise."

"Now, that's more like it." Nick reached over and clapped him on the shoulder, congratulating him. "Did she kiss you back?"

"It was a heat-of-the-moment thing. She'd just gotten a good fright."

"Even in the heat of the moment, you don't make out with someone you have paternal feelings for." Nick was grinning like the Cheshire cat. "She's into you."

"She's made it clear that she doesn't want to be into me. I have to respect that. And I have to respect departmental policy about having a personal relationship with a subordinate."

"You know, you've been divorced from Courtney for ten years. You're a grown man, you're unattached—it's okay for you to have a fling."

"Elise is not the kind of woman you have a fling with."

Nick's knowing nod belied the hushed maturity in his voice. "It's also okay for you to find someone and be happy again."

"There are rules to follow."

"Screw the rules."

George slapped his hand down on the counter. "I am the deputy commissioner of a major metropolitan police department. I'm your boss. I'm her boss. I don't have the option of forgetting the rules."

"Wow." Nick didn't even bat an eye at the rare burst of temper. "That's what they mean by 'it's lonely at the top,' eh?"

George shook his head. "How does Annie put up with you?"

"Slugger loves me. And she knows I love her. I took a bullet for her, George, and I'd do it again. Yeah, we both have blue running through our blood, and it isn't always easy. But we try not to bring our cases home with us, and we make it work." He enunciated that last line to let it sink in. Nick seemed to think there were options for a workplace romance that George knew damn well didn't exist for him. And while

George wished he still had that young man's optimism in him, Nick picked up a set of headphones, turned the light on the target at the end of his lane and pulled out his own weapon. Cradling it in his hands, he urged George to pick up his gun and do the same. "The Glock 9 mil is heavier than the gun you used to carry. Aim down a quarter of an inch or so, and the kick will get you right on the target."

George put on his headphones and took aim beside his nephew.

"We won't let her get hurt."

At least there was one thing they could agree on.

George nodded beside him and squeezed the trigger. "Firing fifteen!"

Chapter Six

Pitsaeli's on the Plaza was well-known for its Italian cuisine, its fine wines and its busy lunch crowd. It wasn't known for its fritzing lights or questionable air-conditioning.

Elise finally gave up pushing her salad around the plate and picked up her napkin to fan herself.

"In Lukinburg, we do not have this unseasonably hot weather." Alexsandr Titov's accent was as melodic as his brother's had been. Noticing her distress, he signaled their waiter and had him top off her glass of ice water. "The sun is bright there. But between the sea and mountains, we have cool breezes. And the air is dry."

Perhaps even more handsome than his older brother had been, Alexsandr's European manners and genteel decorum might have charmed her a couple of years ago. But while she nodded her thanks, she honestly wished George and Quinn would wrap up this meeting and let her step outside onto the Plaza's wide sidewalks to search for an American breeze.

Titov hadn't told them anything useful. He'd apologized more than once for his brother's actions, assured them that his new import/export company was completely legit, and that he was expanding into more than just ammunition manufacturing. He'd even invited George to have KCPD conduct an investigation into his books and business practices. It wasn't as if an intelligent businessman would come right out and ask them for inside information, and since this was a first meeting, it would be inappropriate for Alexsandr to do more than hint that he'd like to become a subsidiary of GSS and sell his defense and survival products to KCPD and other contracts in the Midwest.

Elise had been invited along to today's meeting for one purpose—to see if she recognized Titov's voice or anything else about him that seemed familiar. Unless she could get him to whisper "I love you," or provide a sample of his handwriting, however, there was no way she could confirm that he was the man who'd called her office, left those creepy messages or invaded her home.

And she couldn't bring herself to ask if he knew about the twenty-three roses Nikolai had sent her before his death. She wasn't sure which was more unsettling—having no clue who had developed this obsession with her, or knowing the man terrorizing her was sitting right beside her in a public restaurant.

The lights on the walls flickered again. Elise gasped when they went out for nearly half a minute. For a few seconds the entire restaurant was silent, with only the clinking and clanking and Italian curses coming from the kitchen.

"So sorry, everybody," a thickly accented Italian voice shouted from the kitchen alcove. "I am Arturo Pitsaeli, your host. It is just a blown fuse. We shall have it fixed in moments."

In the spirit of patience and cooperation, the patrons all seemed to be holding their breaths. Soon she heard the drone of electricity surging through the building again. The lights popped back on, and there were cheers from many tables and the crew in the back.

A hand patted her knee beneath the tablecloth and Elise jumped a second time.

"Afraid of the dark?" Alexsandr asked.

After catching the questioning look in George's eyes across the table, she tucked her hair behind her ear, subtly masking the shake of her head, indicating she was all right. "I didn't think I was. Just startled."

She crossed her legs and pulled away from the lingering, unwanted touch as Alexsandr winked a blue eye at her. "One of the items Titov Industrial is developing is a more powerful portable generator. One could run this restaurant during a blackout. Three could run this entire city block." She didn't relax until she saw both his hands on top of the table again. "Perhaps that is something you could use a demonstration for today, yes?"

"Perhaps," she agreed, although she'd warn George and Quinn to stay away from doing business with this man. Her recommendation had nothing to do with business and everything to do with the fact that Alexsandr had just taken his charm over the edge into Creepy Land. She'd like nothing better than to end this meeting and never see another Titov again. And whether it was the language barrier or his propensity to combine business with pleasure, Elise thought the direct approach might be the best way to get the answers they needed from this man. "I don't suppose you know how many roses your brother sent me before he left the country, do you?"

"What?" Alexsandr shook his head. "Nikolai sent you flowers?" He twisted his pinkie ring on his left hand and smiled. "You were very special to him, no?" Elise's left hand fisted around her napkin when he caught the fingers of her right hand and lifted them to his lips for a kiss. "I can see why even my hardheaded brother was charmed by you."

That was no answer at all. Of course, if he did know the significance of twenty-three roses and how they might frighten her, he'd hardly admit to it, would he? She was definitely out of her element on the front line of an investigation like this.

Elise pulled her hand away as quickly as was polite and picked up her purse. "If you gentlemen will excuse me, I need to visit the ladies' room."

All three men rose to their feet when she stood, but she only saw George's stony-gray eyes narrowed with concern before she shook her head and hurried through the path of tables and past the wait stand to the back hallway where the restrooms were located.

After the woman in the stall beside her left, and Elise was alone in the quiet, windowless room, she breathed a noisy sigh of relief. She washed her hands and splashed cool water on her face and neck. Grabbing a towel to blot her skin dry, she looked at herself in the mirror. "Oh, my."

The sleeveless navy blue coatdress and silver

jewelry looked as chic as the day she'd bought them. But no amount of style or makeup could negate the haunted look on her face. She hadn't looked this sleep-deprived since finals week at college. At least those late nights had served a useful purpose. This bone-deep fatigue, the wariness that shadowed her eyes, felt like someone's nefarious plan to wear her down until she caved in to whatever her stalker wanted from her…or she lost her mind.

She quickly tossed the paper towel and opened her purse. Hopefully, a touch of coral lipstick would make her look a little more normal. No wonder George was so worried about her, calling in favors from detectives, crime scene investigators and criminal profilers to solve her little problem. He probably thought she was on the verge of losing all competency as the most trusted member of his staff…and if something didn't change soon, she just might.

Last night she'd showered and gone to bed, thinking exhaustion would claim her and allow her to sleep. But a constant feeling of being watched, of someone lurking in the shadows outside her securely locked windows kept her tossing and turning. Spike's sotto voce growling and suspicious woofs at every little noise hadn't helped her relax, either.

Until she realized there *was* someone watching.

When she peeked through her curtains, she recognized the silver Suburban parked away from the streetlamp outside. As soon as she saw that George Madigan was sitting inside his car, that he was the uninvited presence making her so paranoid, she'd hooked Spike up to his leash, marched outside in her robe and pajamas and kindly asked him to leave.

"You're scaring me."

"Not my intent." He'd climbed out of the car as soon as she'd flipped on the porch light, and met her on the front sidewalk.

When he clamped his hand over her arm and tried to steer her inside, Elise planted her feet. "It's not your responsibility, either."

"It is in more ways than you know."

"What does that mean?"

"It means I'm not going anywhere."

Once she could see it was an argument she wasn't going to win, Elise invited him inside to spend another night on her Chippendale couch. No sense sweating inside his car on the warm summer night, or running his engine all night long just to have air-conditioning. And if she knew exactly where he was, she wouldn't be questioning the presence in the shadows, either.

She didn't suppose her tailored sofa was big

enough for the broad-chested man, nor soft enough to be very comfortable to stretch out on. But she hadn't offered him a guest room upstairs, and he hadn't complained.

In fact, he seemed to be making himself right at home in her house. Although he'd stripped off his jacket, shirt and belt to sleep, he'd placed the gun that he hadn't worn before yesterday beneath the pillow she'd brought down for him.

Her sleep had proved equally fitful as she adjusted to having company in the house. She'd heard him moving around through the house, checking locks, warming up his coffee in the microwave, tussling with Spike when he'd trotted downstairs to check on the noises. Elise wished she could be just as curious and carefree as the dog and go down to George, too. Maybe he'd hold her again. Maybe they'd kiss. Maybe they'd just talk. Maybe then, she'd feel safe enough to let sleep claim her.

Elise drew the lipstick across her mouth, remembering the sensuous pull of George's lips across hers. She remembered every look, every touch.

There were other desires at work, too, plaguing her sleep—the hunger for a man whose masculinity and confident strength were such an integral part of him that he made her feel utterly feminine. It would be easier to fight that forbidden attraction once this mess was cleared up and she could have her normal life back and take care of herself again.

She capped the lipstick and put it away in her purse, just like she had to put away any fantasy she might have about her boss. In another job, in another life, she could see how good she and George might be together. But this was the life she—

The lights in the bathroom suddenly went out. "Oh!"

Elise froze. It was much darker back here than it had been in the dining room, where a bank of windows facing the street had compensated for the blown fuse. Elise heard shouts and the crack of dishes breaking from the kitchen on the other side of the wall, and a rising din of complaints from customers and staff alike. The power must be out throughout the restaurant again.

With her vision struggling to compensate for the near blackout conditions in the restroom, Elise fumbled in the darkness to find something familiar and wound up gripping the edge of the sink, anxiously waiting for the lights to come back on. She waited and waited. A body banged into the hallway wall, and she jumped. A tray of silverware crashed to the floor and someone cursed.

"Why aren't the lights coming back on?" Elise whispered. The air in here was quickly growing stale without the vents and air-conditioning on to filter out the scents of potpourri, oven fumes and something faintly moldy in the background.

Arturo Pitsaeli was shouting again. "Please, everybody, stay in your seats. My apologies. Free gelati for everyone. Please. Sit."

But it didn't sound as if people were listening. Dozens of footsteps and chairs screeching across the terra-cotta tile floors sounded more like people were panicking—or were furious, at least, about the new delay in their lunch break.

The entire fuse box must have blown. This was a complete power outage.

She needed to get out of here. She needed to get to some light.

Elise reached forward until her fingertips butted against the mirror. Turning to her left, she headed toward the exit, trailing her fingers along the smooth glass to orient herself. When her fingers grazed across rougher plaster, her hip bumped into the trash can, knocking it against the wall. She reached out to grab it, but before she could stop its wobbling, the bathroom door opened and a sliver of murky light took the room from opaque to merely dark. "Hold the door, would you? Trust me, it isn't any better in here."

No one answered.

"Hello? Is someone there?"

The blast of noise from the restaurant muted and the blackness returned as the door softly closed again. Maybe whoever had tumbled into the wall outside had accidentally knocked the door open, without coming inside at all.

Elise shook her head and inched forward.

But other senses were arguing with her useless vision. She halted, inhaling a quick breath, imagining a whiff of musky heat in the air. Perspiration? Not hers.

Her pulse thundered in her ears at the deafening silence and she recoiled half a step. "Who's there?"

No reply.

Was her imagination working overtime to create a threat that wasn't there?

Was that…? Yes. The deep, rhythmic whisper of someone breathing.

She wasn't alone.

And her company wasn't talking.

"Who are you?" The darkness swam inside her head and she stumbled back against the sinks. "Answer me!"

Chapter Seven

"Answer me!"

"Elise?" She squealed at the sharp rap against the bathroom door and gave up her blind search for the phone in her purse. The door opened and a broad figure was silhouetted in the dim light. "Are you in here?"

"George?" Relief was so intense, it made her light-headed. "Watch out. There's someone—"

The beam of a small flashlight swung into the room and bounced off the mirror, temporarily blinding her. She turned away.

"Elise!" His familiar grip closed around hers, pulling her to the door. "Let's go. It's Crazy Town out here."

"But—"

"Now."

Squeezing George's hand, she held on as they jostled their way through swarming people and moving chairs. Waiters carried trays with free desserts, patrons tried to pay their checks and depart, and a few, possibly, simply departed to be chased down by the hostess and by Arturo himself.

"Quinn will cover the check," George announced. "I want to get you out of here."

Compared to the pitch-black bathroom, the dusky twilight out here was hard on her eyes. She squinted her lids against the growing brightness as they neared the front windows. But she couldn't forget the smell and the sound in the restroom. She tugged against George's forward momentum. "Where's Mr. Titov?"

"He got a phone call. He was heading to the front door to take it when the lights blew. To be honest, I don't know where he ended up."

Elise planted her feet and got him to stop. "What about the man in the restroom?"

"The what?"

She raised her voice to be heard above the chaos. "There was someone in there with me. I think it may have been him."

"Titov?"

"I don't know. He never said anything."

There was no need to explain why she'd be concerned about company in the restroom. George's eyes hardened like granite and he quickly reversed course. "Come on." When they reached the back hallway, he pushed her

against the wall and bent his knees to bring his
face even with hers. "Wait here. Don't move."
Although she couldn't read his eyes in the shadows, there was no mistaking the frustrated sigh
that matched her own. Before she could even
thank him for believing her implausible story, he
leaned in and pressed a hard, quick kiss against
her mouth and pulled away. "Right here," he reminded her. "I'll be back."

Her hand had barely landed on the silk of his
tie before he was pulling his jacket back, drawing his gun, leaving her. "This is the police. I'm
coming in."

Opening the door, he pushed it all the way
around to the wall, ensuring no one was hiding behind it before bracing his wrists together
to point his gun and flashlight in the same direction. Sweeping the light back and forth, he
went inside and disappeared into the darkness.

Elise's fingers drifted back to touch the tingling stamp of caring and promise that lingered
on her lips. She held her breath, praying as hard
for George to find the silent intruder as she was
for him to avoid any kind of confrontation that
could get him hurt.

She tried to tune her hearing to pinpoint the
soft breathing she'd heard before, but it wasn't
easy. The more she tried to concentrate, the

more distractions there were. The chef was herding his sous chefs and waitstaff out of the kitchen with a flashlight while Arturo Pitsaeli pushed by her in the opposite direction, carrying a broken wine bottle and muttering in Italian. Greenish security lights had come on, casting a weird glow over all their faces, obscuring their expressions into distorted masks.

"Empty. I checked every stall." George holstered his weapon as he shooed the last waitress out of his path. "Checked the men's, too. There's no one there."

Another mystery she couldn't explain? "But he was there. I didn't imagine it. I smelled him."

"He could have easily lost himself in this crowd or slipped out back through the kitchen." George leaned in close enough for her to read the seriousness of his expression. There was no confusion or pity there, only a sense of urgency. "I think distance from here is our best protection right now." He snatched her hand and she willingly hurried into step with him as he led her back into the restaurant. "Let's go."

They reentered the throng that seemed to grow more crowded and less friendly by the second. She was tall in her high heels, but not tall enough to see over George's shoulder or around the patrons standing so close to her. They hurried closer to daylight with every step, but even as Elise's eyes adjusted, there were too many people and too much movement to focus on any one face.

"Maybe it was just one of the waitresses catching a moment of quiet away from the dining room. It may not have been Alexsandr. Or any man." That was the explanation she was going with when George pulled her through the front doors onto the sidewalk outside. She instantly squinted against the bright sun and reached into her bag for her sunglasses. But when she released George's hand and someone pushed her into a mother trying to negotiate a stroller and a crying child through the crowd, she decided it was safer to keep moving with the tide of people pouring out of storefronts and eateries. "Sorry," she apologized, catching the woman's diaper bag and hooking it securely back over her shoulder.

The sidewalk was packed. Not just with the usual spate of summer tourists coming to see the historic Mediterranean architecture, fountains and works of art, but shoppers, lunchtime guests like themselves and personnel from the local businesses. Doors were closing. Gates were coming down over storefront windows. The outdoor dining tables at Pitsaeli's took up half the sidewalk, creating a bottleneck of pedestrians who all seemed to be heading toward the parking lot and garages beyond the next intersection. And where the side streets crossed the wide boulevard, traffic lights were blinking on backup power and a jam of cars was blocking the crosswalks.

George lifted the woman's stroller past the fence surrounding Pitsaeli's sidewalk café, accepted her thanks, then pulled Elise back into step beside him. "Don't talk yourself out of what you saw."

"But I didn't see him. Even when you opened the door that first time, he could have been behind it. She could have been. No one could have—"

"Stop it. I know you. Practical. Levelheaded. Resourceful. I don't think you imagined it for one moment."

"But I haven't been myself lately. You know that, too."

With a grumbling curse, he pulled Elise around the fence as well, into a small pocket empty of humanity for the moment. George stretched his neck above the crowd and looked up and down the street, assessing the situation before pulling out his cell phone. "This is a madhouse. Electricity on the whole block must be out."

He punched in 9-1-1, but they couldn't wait there long. With the hundred-degree temperature, the stucco reflected even more heat. If dots of perspiration were already beading between Elise's breasts in her cotton dress, then George must be boiling in his jacket and tie. Nodding as if he'd read her thoughts, he took her hand again and led her back into the flow of people.

The press of pedestrians was almost suffocating. Despite the slippery heat of their adjoining palms, Elise laced her fingers with George's and held on tighter while he made a call to Dispatch. Raising his voice to a commanding timbre to be heard over the din, he identified himself and ordered street patrol and backup crowd control as well as the utility department into the area pronto.

Spotting a familiar uniformed officer beside his black-and-white cruiser across the street, Elise walked the next several steps on tiptoe and pointed. "That's Denton Hale's partner, Gary Boyd. We can get them to help."

"Good idea." Shifting course, George pulled her around a bronze statue and flowers decorating a planter in the middle of the wide sidewalk.

But her grip loosened as they jostled through the crowd. Someone stepped on her heel. "George?"

With a hop, she tried to keep the leather pump on her toes. But someone elbowed into her side, knocking her off balance, and she lost both George's hand and her right shoe.

"Wait." In a blink they were separated by a family rattling off panicked directions to each other in Chinese or some other Eastern tongue. Panicking a bit herself, she bent down to pick up her shoe. But a man's foot lumbered past, kicking it away into a trample of feet. "Hey!"

"Elise?" She heard George's shout and straightened back up.

She bobbed up and down as the crowd carried her farther from the sound of his voice. She caught a glimpse of his distinctive silver and brown hair and raised her hand over her head so he could see her. "I'm over— Ow!"

A hard shoe ground her bare toes against the concrete. Pain shot through her foot and she nearly toppled over.

"You stupid—"

A gloved hand snagged hers. A voice whispered against her nape. "I'll save you, Elise."

That voice.

"No!" Elise stumbled as the hand dragged her back through the crowd. "Let go of me!"

But the moment she spun around and would have seen his face, he released her or she was knocked free. Several people surged between them, blocking her view. She caromed from one person to the next, some cursing her, some helping, all keeping her from the truth.

"George!" She finally threw herself against the wall of the nearest building. Limping on one shoe, protecting her injured foot, she hugged the wall and inched forward.

When a hand clamped down on her shoulder, she screamed. The crowd retreated from the shrieking woman the way a line of ants swerved to avoid a puddle. But the hand on her arm stayed put. She clawed at the grip.

"Easy. Easy, Miss Brown. Whoa. Are you okay?"

Elise froze. It was a full voice, not that creepy whisper. Blue uniform. Black gloves tucked in front pocket. Bare fingers against her skin.

Panic rushed out on a quick breath and she tilted her chin up to read the apology in Shane Wilkins's green eyes. "Elise?"

"Shane? Thank God it's you."

"I was eating lunch at the sub place down the street when the lights went out and I heard the all call…" His gaze dropped to the ground. "Ma'am, you're bleeding."

The scrapes on her foot were inconsequential. "A man grabbed me. Where's George…the deputy commissioner?"

"Elise!"

He pushed through the edge of the crowd and she threw her arms around his neck. "George!"

"I've got you." His arms latched around her back like a vise and he carried her back to the wall before setting her down. "What's wrong?"

When her feet touched concrete and his hands settled at her waist, she hung on to his lapels and kept him close. "He's here. He just grabbed me."

"I grabbed you, ma'am." Shane threw up his hands in surrender, apologizing again. "Sorry I startled—"

"No. In the crowd… I felt… He said…" Elise peeked between the two men, searching for a face she didn't know in an overwhelming sea of faces. George's body was braced around hers, but she could feel the bumping and pushing.

He brushed aside the hair that stuck to her cheeks. Maybe they were damp from heat. Maybe they were damp from tears. Either way, those stone-gray eyes didn't seem to like what they saw. "We're getting out of here. Can you walk?"

Elise managed a jerky nod before George

tucked her to his side. She willingly wound her arm around his waist beneath his suit jacket, clinging tightly to the belt beside the holster he wore. What little strength she had left ebbed into his and he half led, half carried Elise straight into the swarm of pedestrians. His body was a shield that protected her from figments of her imagination and the crazy mash-up of hot, sweaty bodies filing past.

"Wilkins, can you take point and get us across the street to the parking garage?" George didn't wait for a confirmation before his shoulder shifted beneath her cheek and he waved to another officer on the scene. "Hale, we need your help."

The ground suddenly dropped from beneath her feet and she clutched at George's chest. When her bare foot grazed against hot asphalt, she understood that George had lifted her to step off the curb and carry her across the street. She felt a hand on her elbow and turned. Denton Hale's face swam in and out of focus above his blue collar. Maybe she was suffering delirium from heatstroke.

"Is she all right?" He looked from George to her as he helped her cross the street. "Ma'am, you look mighty pale."

"She'll be fine." With a boost onto his hip,

George took her full weight and climbed over the concrete median. "Wilkins. Clear that entrance. I'm on the first floor, third row in. Hale, get those cars out of the intersection."

"Yes, sir." The officers answered in tandem, rushing away in a blur of blue and a hail of shouts and whistles.

"This way, sir." Shane waved them forward, scattering the people gathered at the entrance to the parking garage. "Move along. This is a police emergency. Coming through."

The relative coolness when they reached the shady side of the boulevard revived Elise a little. "I can walk," she offered.

"I know." Although he eased her feet down to the ground, he never relinquished his hold around her waist or slowed his pace. "My car's back there."

"Got it, sir." After George hit the remote to unlock it, Shane opened the door and George lifted her inside behind the steering wheel.

A sharp whistle drew her attention to the street. "Let's move it!" Denton Hale tapped the hood of a car and waved it on through the intersection, clearing the lane in front of the garage exit. When his gaze met hers through the windshield of George's Suburban, he touched the brim of his cap in a salute to her and Elise nodded her thanks.

Meanwhile George was dismissing Officer Wilkins. "You'd better go assist with crowd control, son. Make sure that utility truck gets through."

"I will, sir. Ma'am." He, too, acknowledged Elise before jogging back to the entrance.

"You have good people working for you."

"I do." When George climbed in behind the wheel, Elise scooted across to the passenger seat. The effort seemed to drain the last bit of energy out of her and she sagged against the tan upholstery. Her eyes felt gritty, unfocused. George reached over to pull her purse off her shoulder and drop it to the floorboards at her feet before starting the engine and turning on the air. "There's only one employee I'm worried about right now."

"He touched me. He was in the bathroom with me when the lights went out. And in the crowd, in those few seconds you and I got separated, he grabbed my hand and…" She looked down at her hand as if it were an anathema. "He whispered my name."

She was vaguely aware of George sliding across the seat. Or maybe he was pulling her closer, because he lifted the offending hand onto his thigh and rubbed it between both of his, blotting out the memory of another man's touch. "Can you describe him for me? Do you remember anything about him?"

She'd heard. She'd felt. But she hadn't seen anyone.

A tear spilled over and burned a path down her cheek.

"I'm not crazy. He was there."

"It's okay. We'll figure it out." He wiped away the tear with the pad of his thumb and leaned in to kiss her temple. "We'll find the answers we need."

But when he pulled away, Elise felt a moment of such profound loss that she snatched at his jacket to keep him beside her. She palmed his tie and collar and the strong column of his neck before grasping his jaw between her hands. She looked deep into those handsome eyes, traced the firm line of his mouth with her thumbs, slipped her fingers through the silky salt-and-pepper of his hair and came back to frame his warm skin again. "You're real, aren't you, George? I see you. I can touch you. I hear your voice."

"Yeah, honey, I'm real." The lines beside his eyes deepened as he offered her a reassuring smile. His chest expanded with a steadying breath before he brushed aside a lock of her hair and tucked it behind her ear. He turned his lips into her palm and pressed a ticklish kiss there. "Do you feel me? Do you feel this? I'm right here. And I'm not going anywhere."

He wiped away the next tear that fell, and the next. And then he stroked the pad of his thumb across her mouth, urging it to open, giving her a taste of her own salty tears when her tongue darted out to soothe her sensitized lips. If this tenderness was a figment of her imagination... Her eyes filled with sorrowful tears. "George? I need..."

With a groan that vibrated through the air between them, George leaned in to replace his thumb with his mouth. His lips moved deliberately over hers, sampling, healing, demanding. He thrust his tongue into her mouth, giving her a taste of the rich cappuccino he'd drunk after their meal. He threaded his fingers into her hair, branding her with his hands and mouth as he angled her head back against the seat and moved his body into hers.

The encompassing heat seeping into every pore shocked her to her senses. With an answering hum in her throat, she slid her fingers across his crisp hair to clasp them behind his neck and pull herself further into his kiss.

She opened deeply for him, danced her tongue against his. Catching her bottom lip in a soft nibble, he held her in place as he dragged his hands from her hair, skimming them down her body. Her small breasts leaped beneath the lace of her bra and her properly tailored dress to thrust into the heat of his palms. And when his thumbs teased the tips into hardened pearls, she cried out at the arrows of pure wicked heat firing deep into the heart of her.

George moved his lips to the gasps and hums in her throat, and discovered a sensitive bundle of nerves along her collarbone that elicited a low, keening cry. "Your skin is so soft and pretty," he murmured, kissing his way up the side of her neck to capture a lobe and its silver earring between his teeth.

His skin was tempting, too. Like fine sand beneath her fingertips in some places, like smooth silk in others. Always warm to the touch. And far too covered up.

Eager to explore his body, Elise fought with his tie. She slid the knot down his chest and unhooked some buttons on his shirt, slipping her hands inside to singe her fingers on the musky heat of his chest.

When he reclaimed her mouth, she willingly gave him everything he asked for. He slid his hand along her thigh and hooked it behind her knee to pull her into his chest, forcing her to wind her arms around his neck and straddle his lap. His lips continued to work their magic against her mouth and skin, kindling fires with every kiss and sweep of his hands. And if he wanted to do something about the bulge swelling behind his zipper, she wouldn't stop him.

This man was her lifeline to sanity, her feelings for him the only thing that made sense in her senseless world.

This was the passion that had been simmering beneath the surface of protocol and past mistakes for too long. These were the emotions that went far beyond friendship and respect. This was the want, the need, the love she felt for this man.

The love she shouldn't feel.

The love that would surely guarantee her another broken heart.

The love that was as overwhelming and fragile and impossible to hold on to as the certainty she would walk away from this mess with her wits intact.

"George," she whispered, dragging her mouth from his. "We need to stop. You know we shouldn't... I'm okay now."

"Maybe I'm not." He hugged her to his chest

for several moments, each of them breathing deeply, quickly.

She could feel his heart thumping against her breast as strongly as she felt her own. Her thoughts were clear now, and she was aware enough to know that she'd climbed into his lap in a public parking garage, giving in to a desire that simply couldn't be. She was also smart enough to know that the terror hounding her might be at bay for the moment, but it was by no means gone from her life.

Easing her grip on his neck, Elise leaned back to frame his face and give that handsome mouth one last kiss before she crawled off him and back to her seat. "We can't do this, George. As much as I want to, I can't. There are too many things that could go wrong...."

"Too many ways you could get hurt." He tucked a mussed lock of hair behind her ear and nodded. "Hurting you is the last thing I want to do."

He slid back behind the steering wheel, taking a few moments to straighten his clothes, although he ended up pulling his tie off completely and leaving the top button of his shirt open. "You make me feel like I'm twenty again." He shook his head and shifted the car into Reverse. "And sometimes like I'm a hundred and twenty."

She hugged herself, trying to calm all the nerve endings still sparking with the electricity of their embrace. Yes, George was older than she was, but she'd never considered him old. His age had never been the reason she'd kept her distance. "If a crazy woman's opinion matters, I'd say you're just right."

That earned her half a laugh and a little less guilt.

"Buckle up, Goldilocks." He pulled a magnetic light from beneath his seat and stuck it on the roof of the car. Then he punched the siren a couple of times to clear a path and pulled the big vehicle into the bumper-to-bumper traffic as if they were the missing piece completing a puzzle.

Elise was emotionally exhausted and physically weary. Her scraped-up toes were throbbing and the loss of George's abundant body heat left her feeling chilled. And despite Denton Hale waving them on through the intersection, she felt trapped. She was a prisoner in her beloved city, at the mercy of a man who seemed to know her every move and delight in staying one step ahead of her. He knew where she lived, where she worked, where she ate and, quite possibly, how much the man beside her meant to her.

If her stalker's plan was to wear down her mental and emotional strength and make her vulnerable to whatever influence he wanted to have over her, then he was succeeding. If he thought he was having some twisted kind of relationship with her, expressing true love, then he was even sicker than she felt at the moment.

Despite another *whoop-whoop* of the siren and the flashing lights, there was still a logjam of pedestrians and traffic, making it difficult to get out of the Plaza area.

"Do you think he did this?" she asked, glancing out the window at the thinning crowd and dark, closed-up businesses.

"Caused the power outage and the panic?" George nodded to Shane Wilkins as the young cop held up a line of traffic so they could pass. Had he or Hale or anyone else seen that make out session in the front seat of their boss's car? Would they dare gossip about it? Would George care if they did? Should she care about compromising her position in the deputy commissioner's office any further? "At the very least he was following you and took advantage of the opportunity. I'll call Cliff Brandt to have him tell me exactly what caused the lights to go out and have Nick check alibis on Alexsandr Titov and James Westbrook."

"I'll mark it on your calendar as soon as we get back to the office."

"I'm not taking you to HQ, Elise."

She glanced across the car, seeing the look that allowed no argument on his stern features. No. She didn't suppose she was in any shape to do her job right now.

"You're safe," George assured her, reaching across the seat to squeeze her hand. "We'll get through this. Together."

She nodded and held on tight, not quite believing him.

Chapter Eight

Elise drew the thin brush along the groove in the window's top casing, evening out the white trim that would frame her navy blue shutters. After this second coat dried, she'd be ready for hardware and installation. She held on to the top of the stepladder and leaned back to evaluate her work.

"Are you going to do this all night long?"

Back in her own house, amongst her own things, with her own familiar routine, Elise was feeling a sense of relatively peaceful normalcy, considering the afternoon she'd had, and didn't startle at the low-pitched voice teasing her. She even smiled when she turned to see the deputy commissioner of KCPD leaning against the archway into the living room, with his fingers hooked into the front pockets of his faded jeans. Those gray eyes were focused on her bare legs beneath the edge of her cutoff shorts, well south of the face he was communicating with. Spike, who had traitorously seemed to prefer making friends with their new guest than spending time with her, trotted past George into the room and jumped onto the couch.

"Are you going to stay on your phone all night?" she teased right back. "Is that how you spend all your evenings after a full day at work? Doing more work?" She glanced over to the black dog, pawing at the protective tarp and cushions beneath to make himself a comfy bed. "Good grief, you've even worn out Spike."

George's gaze dutifully kicked up to hers and walked into the room. "I offered to help."

Maybe having George Madigan in her home was beginning to feel a little too normal. She'd never seen him dressed so casually before. But when she'd come downstairs in her paint shirt, shorts and flip-flops two hours earlier, he'd changed into a pair of wrinkled jeans and a gray KCPD T-shirt pulled from a duffel bag in the back of the Suburban he'd parked in the driveway behind her Explorer.

He was still wearing his gun and badge, still moved with the same authoritative bearing—still looked like a man in charge. But this version of her boss was one who was a little more approachable, one who could patiently clean and bandage a scraped foot, and didn't seem to mind

Chinese takeout at the kitchen counter for dinner, or a dog napping under his chair while he sat in Elise's home office across the foyer to make phone calls.

Realizing she'd been staring as overtly as he had, Elise turned back to the window to dab at a couple more spots. The man who'd rescued her from that madness this afternoon, then nearly seduced her back to her senses, had been heroic and irresistible, larger-than-life and strictly off-limits. But the man strolling through her living room tonight didn't seem like the forbidden boss in a suit and tie. This guy seemed like someone she could meet anywhere, a man whose sense of duty, caring and sexy confidence would have turned her head instantly. This was a man she would have willingly looked forward to spending time with and getting to know better.

That made her attraction to this George Madigan even more dangerous than the man she had already fallen for. Elise knew how to follow rules and do what was expected of her. She wasn't so certain about following her heart and trusting fate to lead her to a happily ever after.

She wiped her brushes on the rag hanging over the top of the stepladder. "It's good therapy for me. Fixing up things, taking care of them. It makes me feel like I'm accomplishing something worthwhile. I like the idea of preserving something that was once important to someone else. It's good, honest work, the physical activity gives me time to think and, of course, I love the beautiful results."

George's hands closed around her waist to help her down. "There's nothing broken about you, Elise."

"So now you're my therapist, too?" She moved away from both his distracting touch and discomfiting words, kneeling down on the drop cloth to put the two brushes into a tin can she'd saved.

"I'm just a man who calls things like I see them." He handed her the rubber mallet from atop the sawhorses after she'd replaced the lid on the paint can. "You've had bad things happen to you, but that doesn't mean it's your fault they happened. You don't have to fix everyone and everything because of some penance you think you owe."

She hammered the can shut with a little more force than usual. "So what makes me such a magnet for the weirdos and users of the world, then?"

"You're bighearted. You put others before yourself. You're too kind to not listen to a problem or try to help."

Elise picked up the can and pushed to her feet. "In other words, I'm a doormat."

"In other words—" he plucked the can of paint from her hand and set it on the sawhorse table "—you're a kind, caring woman who sees where she can make a difference in people's lives, and does."

Not fair. She valued his appreciation of her efficiency and dedication on the job—she needed him to respect her abilities there. But between her experience with Nikolai and this crazy stalker, she was barely keeping her personal life together. Getting to know this surprisingly tender, supportive side of the tough, no-nonsense man she worked with every day was making it even harder to remember they should never be more than friends. "I appreciate you volunteering to keep an eye on the place, sir. But I don't need a pep talk."

As expected, George bristled and backed away a step at her use of the formality. It felt like a cheap shot, but if she didn't learn to keep her distance from him soon, she never would.

"Sorry if I overstepped the boundaries of your hospitality, Miss Brown." Miss Brown? Was that rankling punch in the gut how calling him sir made him feel? Elise's gaze shot up to his, but George's eyes had hardened like stone again. He propped his hands at his waist beside his gun and badge, reminding them both of the real reason he was here. "I spent most of my time on the phone with my nephew and the crime lab tonight. According to Nick, Titov's only alibi is that he was stuck in the crowd at the Plaza, like us, until his driver picked him up around 1:35 p.m. Westbrook says he was at the ball game at Kauffman Stadium, but Nick is looking for more than a ticket stub to prove it. The game lasted over three hours, so that would be plenty of time to leave and get to the Plaza and get back to his seat."

Elise slipped back into assistant mode, although she wasn't sure where the glum mood was coming from. This professional relationship was all she wanted with George, wasn't it? "And the power outage? Did Mr. Brandt have any answers for you?"

"There was a transformer that blew the power grid in that area. His preliminary analysis indicates something was misaligned and it couldn't handle the peak demand. But whether that misalignment was human error or deliberate sabotage, he can't tell yet."

"I don't suppose there's good news from the lab, either?"

George shrugged. "Annie pulled a DNA profile off the envelope flap, but she hasn't found anything to match it to yet."

"Can she expand her search worldwide? Maybe Mr. Titov's profile will show up in a foreign database."

"Or Westbrook's. You said he worked abroad for several years." She nodded. "I've already got her working on it." Then George's chest expanded with a deep breath, a sure sign she wasn't going to like his next bit of information. "Our perp has upped his game. Sending gifts and love notes isn't enough for him anymore. Now he wants to make contact."

Elise hugged her arms around her waist, staving off a sudden chill. "Your garden-variety sicko. How did I get so lucky?"

"If Titov or Westbrook or whoever was trying to get to you this afternoon, then their plan failed. I don't know if that was an attempted kidnapping or something worse. But since isolating you in an unruly crowd didn't work—"

"He'll try again."

George simply nodded.

Since there was nothing more to discuss that wouldn't hurt one or the other's feelings, or make Elise feel they were no closer to identifying the man whose twisted idea of love was poisoning her life, she picked up the can with the paint-filled brushes and circled around George. "It's getting late. I'd better clean my brushes and clear up some of this mess so you have a place to sleep tonight."

Spike hopped off the couch and followed her through the kitchen into the garage. Despite the cool formality that had resumed between them, George followed her out to the utility sink. While she washed out the brushes, he and the dog inspected the storage shelves and the antique furniture and doors waiting to be stripped and restained or painted. Those were projects for cooler weather when she could open the garage door for plenty of ventilation.

But while Spike flushed out a black cricket to do battle with, George tapped his fingers against the old glass in the door to the backyard. The whole thing shook in its frame when he jimmied the knob.

"I don't suppose I should tell you that's an antique," she cautioned.

He pulled a paint-chipped oak dresser in front of it to reinforce the exit. "And I don't suppose I should tell you that even your little poodle monster there could break through this door if he wanted to. It's not secure enough."

"An intruder would have to get through the door into the kitchen, too."

He shook his head. "That one's not any better. We should have replaced all the locks when you got the front door changed."

Elise's chin dropped to her chest in a weary sigh. "Are you trying to make me feel safer? Because you're failing miserably."

He didn't answer until he stood right beside her. "I have never lied to you, Elise. And I'm not going to start now." He turned off the water and rescued the brushes that were long past clean, shaking them off and hanging them up on the hook over the sink. "I don't know what we're up against exactly, yet. But I'm doing everything I know how to keep you safe." He turned on the water again and picked up the bar of soap, sudsing it up before he pulled her hands beneath the warm spray and cleaned the stains from her fingers. "I'll admit that I'm a little out of my element—I've been pushing papers for too long. I'm not sure I'll see the bad guy coming."

"George, I didn't mean that you weren't capable—"

"Hush." The warmth from the water and his gentle, purposeful hands were taking the edge off her fears and fatigue. "I'm old enough I don't need my ego stroked. I may be a step or two slower than I once was. But I'm smarter. I'm a hell of a lot more patient. And I guarantee you that, no matter what happens between you and me, I will never give up until this guy is caught or dead and out of your life. I want my old friend back."

By the time he'd turned off the water and was reaching for paper towels, Elise was resting her head against his shoulder. "I'll keep fighting, too."

"We make a good team. Always have." He dipped his lips to kiss her temple. "Don't let him get into your head. We're gonna beat this guy." George moved away when she took over drying her own hands. "I'll check the rest of the house, make sure everything is bolted down for the night."

Elise nodded. "I'll put Spike out for his nightly constitutional. If he doesn't run around and stake things out now, he'll be waking me before dawn to relieve himself."

"I don't want you outside by yourself."

Elise nudged him toward the kitchen door. "All I'm doing is opening the door to the deck and putting him in the backyard. He can run around for a few minutes while I make up one of the guest rooms upstairs. Unless you prefer the hard couch?"

"Wherever you're most comfortable with me is fine."

She'd be most comfortable with everything going back to the way it had been before she'd gotten those twenty-three roses. But since that wasn't an option, Elise called Spike and they followed George into the house where he locked the door behind them. "Spikey, *outside?*"

Understanding the word that meant checking smells and running free, the dog charged straight to the back door and danced in anticipation until Elise turned on the porch light and opened the door. A gust of wind blew some flying dust into her eyes, stinging them shut. By the time she blinked them clear of the debris, Spike had leaped down the steps into the grass and disappeared into the darkness beyond. She caught the tendrils of hair whipping about her face and tucked them behind her ears, holding them in place while she turned her gaze up to the sky. The stars were dim dots of light behind the clouds that moved quickly across the sky, and the moon was nonexistent.

Rain would be a welcome respite after so many days of record-setting heat. But the yawning moans from the thick branches of her elm trees catching the wind warned her that it wasn't any gentle, reviving rain headed their way.

"Do your business fast, sweetie," she said as

another, cooler gust rippled through her baggy paint shirt.

Retreating from the gusting breeze, Elise stepped back inside and locked the door behind her. She jogged up the stairs and turned on the radio in her bedroom, cranking the volume to hear the weather report while she gathered sheets from the linen closet and went into the room next to hers to make up the bed.

"…tornado watch until 1:00 a.m." The announcer talked about cold fronts pushing high pressure systems out of the area as well as other scientific data. Elise attuned her ears to the most pertinent information. "…80 percent chance of rain tonight…possibility of severe weather tomorrow."

Elise turned on the ceiling fan to draw cooler air from the window air conditioners. By the time she'd fluffed the last pillow and set out a fresh towel for George, the announcer had moved into his public service announcement spiel. "The city power district and emergency response teams recommend stocking up on batteries, flashlights, portable lanterns and other supplies. In the event of a tornado, go to your basement or to the innermost, windowless room—"

Elise shut off the radio and headed back down

to let Spike in. Having grown up in the Midwest, she knew the safety procedures by heart. As she passed the archway at the bottom of the stairs, she looked in to see George pacing beside her desk, on his cell phone again. Judging by the snippets of conversation on his end, he knew about the coming storm, too, and was verifying that KCPD's emergency teams would be ready to respond if needed.

When he paused midconversation to make eye contact, she pointed down the hallway to the back door, indicating her destination. With a nod, he returned to his conversation and Elise smiled. The people of Kansas City were in better hands than they knew with men like George Madigan in charge of their safety. She was lucky that he'd made it his personal mission to keep her safe, too.

Knowing he had everything he needed to do his job, just like at the office, Elise left him to his work.

This time, she braced herself for the wind when she opened the back door and whistled. "Spike? Come on in, boy."

Lightning flashed in the clouds overhead, lighting up the backyard for a split second. She waited in the doorway for several seconds before whistling again. "Here, boy!"

Thunder rumbled in ominous portent of the coming storm. "Spike?"

Normally, the dog ran in as soon as she called, anxious to be rewarded with a treat or a tummy rub. Maybe the wind was carrying her voice away from him. But that's what those sharp ears were for, weren't they? "Spike? I've got a treat."

Lightning strobed within the clouds, briefly illuminating the trail of tiny red paw prints crossing back and forth across the deck. Elise shivered with the answering thunder. Where was the dog? "Spike!"

She ran to the railing and peered into the shadows beyond the deck. She heard a snuffling noise off to her right and caught a glimpse of movement beneath the spirea bushes. "Spike?"

Elise hurried off the deck. "Sweetie, are you okay?"

The dog was digging furiously in the dirt. She dropped to her knees and reached beneath the bushes. She slipped her palm beneath his chest, intending to lift him away from the prize he was burying. But when she touched his warm belly, she felt something wet and sticky in his hair. "Sweetie?"

She pulled back her hand. The lightning flashed.

Blood.

Elise screamed.

Throwing herself belly down in the grass, she reached beneath the bush to grab her beloved pet and pull him into her arms.

"Elise!"

She heard loud steps on the deck behind her. Elise rolled onto her bottom, cradling Spike in her arms, stroking his back, checking every limb. He scooted up her chest to lick her chin. His heart thumped rapidly beneath her hands. But there was enough blood to turn his black coat a muddy brown. "Sweetie, what happened? Where are you hurt?"

"Elise? Damn it. I told you not to go outside." She saw the silhouette of a man with a gun in her peripheral vision and instantly recoiled. A light swept through the backyard, but the bright beam settled on the bundle in her arms and George was kneeling beside her. "What happened?"

Recognizing their savior, she grabbed a handful of George's T-shirt and pulled him closer, leaving a red handprint on the cotton, and probably one on her own cheek, too, as she wiped away tears. "We have to help him. That creep's done something to Spike. There's so much blood."

George tucked the gun into the back of his

belt and cupped his hand beneath her elbow to help her stand. "Come on. We have to get you back in the house. Wait a minute." He swung the flashlight to the ground and went down on one knee. He pulled a crumpled piece of paper from the dirt where Spike had been burying it. "What the hell?"

Elise tugged on George's belt. "Hurry. We have to get him to the vet."

"Right. Inside." With the first drops of rain pelting them, they ran back into the house.

Elise went straight to the kitchen, snatching her purse off the counter and heading for the front door. "Can you drive? You're parked behind me."

"Elise, wait." George met her in the foyer, pushing the door she'd just opened shut and turning on the light overhead.

She reached for the knob, but George blocked her path. "Damn it, George, he could go into shock."

He swiped a finger across the stain on his shirt, then touched it to his tongue and spat it out. "Let me see the dog."

"Fine. I'll drive." She gently lay Spike in George's arms and pulled out her keys. But he still wouldn't budge.

"He's not hurt. It's red paint. Like your front

door. Honey, it's paint. He's fine." Spike braced his front paw on George's chest, leaving two more prints. George pulled each leg up and squeezed his paws. There was no squeal of pain, no sign of lethargy, no visible wounds. "See? Just four dirty paws in need of a bath."

"I don't understand." She dropped her purse on the floor and swept her hands over the dog, petting, double-checking. Elise's world rocked on its axis. She'd been so certain Spike was hurt, so devastated that the man from the Plaza had abused her pet, maybe even tried to kill her most loyal friend. But now it was some kind of sick joke? "How did he get into the paint? I keep it in the garage when I'm not using it. And I haven't had the red out for months." She pulled a torn shred of paper from the clasp on Spike's collar. "What's this?"

George folded his hand around hers, heedless of the paint they were transferring. "I need you to sit down."

"Why?" She looked up into George's eyes. Lightning flashed through the windows behind him, and he didn't so much as blink. He knew something. "What is it? Did he do this to Spike? Was he here?"

He nodded toward the stairs. "Sit."

"No. Tell me." She saw the dusty piece of

paper stuffed into the front pocket of his jeans. Elise pulled it out before he guessed her intent.

"Elise."

"This was attached to Spike's collar." The torn scrap in her hand fit the missing corner of the paper the dog had been burying in the yard. She read the note. Elise's world swayed and George's strong hand guided her to the stairs where he sank down beside her on the second step. The last bit of fight left in her surrendered.

Next time, the blood will be real. You should have listened to me. I don't want to hurt you or the things you love, but I need you to understand how much you hurt me. I saw you kiss him. I can forgive you a second time. But never again. You and I have something special. Once we are together, I'll make you understand.
I Love You, Elise.

A boom of lightning shook the walls, but she barely heard it. "Here." She pushed the note into George's hand. "This is evidence. You'll need to give it to your nephew. I assume you'll be calling him."

"Elise?"

She had nothing left. No energy. No hope. No

fear. No memory of love or happiness or relief or regret. There was work to do and responsibilities to manage. But she felt…nothing.

She scooped Spike from George's arms and hugged him against her chest. "Give him to me. I'll go start a bath."

GEORGE STOOD IN the darkness on the second-floor landing, looking through the doorway into Elise's bedroom to watch her sleep. Or try to, at least.

She'd left the lamp on beside her bed and was dozing in fitful starts on top of the quilt, touching the dog, who rested against the curve of her stomach, each time she awoke. Even the storm that cocooned the house in a steady drumbeat of rain and cooled the humid temperatures to a tolerable level couldn't coax her into a restful slumber.

He wasn't in much better shape. It was tearing him up inside to see her like this—a pale, numbed automaton who couldn't even dredge up a smile for the spoiled mutt she loved so much.

George had changed into the button-down shirt he'd worn earlier in the day and tossed his paint-stained T-shirt into a plastic bag in case there was any useful evidence on it the department could use. He scraped his palm over the stubble of his late-night beard, masking a weary sigh before turning to his nephew. "Has the storm washed away any chance of finding this bastard?"

"There's no trail to follow. No cars in the neighborhood that don't belong here." Although he'd hung his KCPD rain slicker on the hook inside Elise's back door to dry, Nick's wet hair was slicked to his scalp and dripping tiny dark circles on the shoulders of his black T-shirt. "I bagged the paint can I found under the bushes. It's the same brand as the others in the garage."

George suspected as much. "He probably took that, too, when he broke in before."

"I'll have Annie check the can and the letter at the lab." Like George's, Nick's voice was barely more than a whisper. "There were depressions in the grass that looked like shoe prints—bigger than mine. Looks like he came into the yard through the side gate." Nick tucked his phone back into the pocket of his jeans. "I took a picture of the shoe prints, but anything else out there is a puddle of mud now. He probably lured the dog out to him with the treats we found underneath those white-flowered bushes, then attached the note to his collar and dumped the paint on him to freak her out."

"It worked. She's exhausted, but she wouldn't take a sedative." Elise was lying in there in the same baggy paint shirt and cutoff shorts she'd had on earlier. Spike had been thoroughly bathed and was drying off on her clothes and quilt top. "She just wants to hold the dog."

Nick squeezed a hand over George's shoulder. "Well, then you try to get some rest. I'm parked out front. I'll keep an eye on things for a while. I called Spencer, too." Nick's partner had just been promoted to lieutenant and would probably be moving into more administrative duties like George soon. But until then, he couldn't think of two better detectives to back him up on any case. "Spence is going to track down where Alexsandr Titov and Westbrook have been this evening. He's coming over after that, too, to help keep an eye on things. We'll make sure nothing else happens tonight."

"Thanks, Nick." George tore his watchful gaze away from Elise long enough to give his nephew a hug. "Tell Spencer thanks, too."

After patting each other's backs, Nick pulled away. "Spence asked me why you didn't call him in sooner. He thinks of you like family and would have volunteered his time on this investigation in a heartbeat."

George shoved his hands into the pockets of

his jeans and nodded. "I know. At first I was trying to respect Elise's request to stay out of it. When I realized I had to get involved, that I was losing her to these mind games, I knew we were short staffed and I couldn't assign anyone to an unofficial case—not with tempers so high around the department and money so tight." His shoulders lifted with a weary sigh. "And maybe part of me wanted to see if I could still be the cop I needed to be without calling in any favors at all."

"I don't see you missing a beat, old man. The evidence we've got against this guy is starting to stack up. Terroristic threats, attempted kidnapping, burglary. All we need is the perp to match that DNA to, and you can put this guy away for a long time."

George grunted a wry laugh. "All we need…"

Another beat of silence passed. "You want to tell me again how this isn't personal for you?"

George glanced down at the young detective beside him. Maybe not so young anymore, because Nick's instincts were right on target. "It's personal."

After a decisive nod, Nick headed down the stairs like a man on a mission, disappearing into the darkness of the house's first floor. A few seconds later, George heard the downpour of rain and rumbles of thunder when the front door opened and locked again, leaving him and Elise alone in the house.

George stood there in the shadows several seconds longer, absorbing the quiet of the rain and the night, letting Mother Nature's healing power seep into his blood and smooth the rough edges of his protective anger before he moved to stand in Elise's doorway. From the bandages on her bare toes to the waves of dark hair that had kinked up with the rain and fanned over the pillow behind her head, Elise Brown was a thing of beauty. He'd probably been half in love with her for a long time. But the rules and regulations had never let him think of her as anything more than the woman his office couldn't live without.

Now he was trying to resolve himself to the fact that he, the man, couldn't live without her, either.

"I could hear you out there, talking." Elise's voice was soft, but not drowsy. Still, she never lifted her head from the pillow. "Is Nick going to stay?"

George stepped into the room, winking to the dog when he raised his head. Spike settled right back down against Elise, as if the dog was smart enough to know what the reassurance meant, or he was simply that comfortable with having George around. "He's parked out front. He and his partner will watch the house tonight."

"Good. I hope you can get some sleep, then."

She still had her back to him, but George wasn't making any secret of his intent. He untied his shoes and toed them off. "Neither one of us can afford another night without much sleep."

"I know."

He unhooked his belt and removed his gun and badge, setting them all on the table beside her bed before turning off the lamp.

"I'm not sleeping next door, Elise." He sat on the edge of the bed, resting his palm on the curve of her hip. The fact that she didn't startle at his touch spoke to her fatigue. Or maybe to something else.

"I don't want you that far away. I need you to stay."

"I need to stay," he echoed in unison.

At last, she rolled onto her back and looked at him. In the flashes of light from the storm outside, he could see the crystallized remnants of tears that had dried on her skin. "Don't be my boss tonight, okay? Just be George Madigan."

With a nod, he lay down beside her on top of the quilt. She turned onto her side and he circled his arm around her waist, pulling her close, spooning her back against his chest. Her bottom nestled against his groin and their legs tangled together. George found a comfortable spot for his head on her pillow, and wrapped both Elise and her dog in his arms.

A shared sigh of rightness, of finally being where they needed to be, merged them tightly together, with only the clothes they wore keeping them apart. "I want to fight this guy, George," Elise whispered. "But I don't know if I'm strong enough."

"Tomorrow you will be. We'll both be strong enough."

George kissed her neck, then buried his nose in the silk of her hair and let sleep claim them both.

Chapter Nine

Elise pushed her hair off her face and opened her eyes to the sunshine glowing behind the curtains on her windows. The deep, dreamless sleep was hard to shake off, and it took her a few moments to orient herself.

Her bedroom.

The sun was up.

Rain stopped.

Heat wave had returned.

Her arms were empty.

Instantly waking to full alertness, she patted the bed beside her. "Spike?"

"Shh. He's okay."

When she tried to roll over, the vise around her waist anchored her in place. But the deep whisper against her ear was clear—as was the explanation for her body being so toasty warm.

"Don't worry." George's lips stirred the hair at her nape. His husky morning voice hummed into her ear. "Nick is walking him outside. I had him give Spike some fresh water and food, too."

Spike was okay. She could drift back to sleep.

Or not.

Was there a cell in her body that wasn't suddenly aware of the man holding her?

George was spooned against her back. She could feel his chest pushing into her with every breath. She felt soft denim against the bare skin of her leg, his muscular thigh draped over both of hers, their toes touching.

His hand was tucked possessively beneath her shirt, his fingertips teasing the elastic that curved beneath her breast, her palm layered over his on the outside of the old cotton shirt that still smelled faintly of wet dog. Even now, she matched her fingers to his, as if she'd welcomed the intimacy of his warm hand on her skin and was holding on to keep him from moving away.

Had they slept together like this all night?

Elise pulled her hand away. "I'm sorry. I didn't realize I was that much of a cuddler."

"I'm not complaining." When she shifted to put some proper distance between them, his fingers splayed across her belly and his grip tightened. "But don't move for a couple of seconds, okay?"

"Need a minute to wake up?" She studied the sunshine creeping in behind the curtains to warm her delicately striped wallpaper. "It's going to be hot again today. After only one night of rain. It'll probably make the humidity even worse. I wonder if we'll get those storms the weatherman predicted today." When she realized she was rambling like a nervous schoolgirl, she reminded herself she was a full-grown woman and should start acting like it. With her brain more awake than it had been a minute ago, she started considering the possible reasons for George's request. Her first instinct had her tugging at his wrist and trying to sit up. "I'm sorry. Did your arm go to sleep? I've been lying on it all night, haven't—?"

"Elise—"

"Is something wrong…?" But her squirming only drove her bottom into the juncture between his thighs and she felt the unmistakable bulge of his arousal butting against her. Elise went still. "Oh."

But suddenly, every nerve in her body tingled in anticipation, chasing away the last dregs of her heavy sleep.

George moved his hand to the jut of her hip to gently force a little distance between them. "I don't know if I was trying to save you from embarrassment. Or me. Nothing has to happen. I just need a minute to…get comfortable again."

"You don't want something to happen?"

His chest-deep groan stirred the hair at her nape. He pressed a soft nip to the juncture of her neck and shoulder, and every eager nerve seemed to rush to the spot. "This is what we need to discuss," he whispered against her skin, his very breath another caress that raised goose bumps across her skin. "Oh, I don't just mean the obvious reaction I'm having to you. But how good we are when we're together. At the office. As friends. When we're close like this. Somewhere along the line, you turned being indispensable into being…irresistible."

Elise reached down to lace her fingers together with the hand on her hip. "I thought you were the irresistible one."

"Now you're just stroking an old man's ego."

A touch of ire blended with the desire waking inside her. Keeping their fingers entwined, she lifted his hand from her shorts and carefully adjusted herself to roll over onto her back and look up into gray eyes that had darkened into granite this morning. "I wouldn't do that. One, I don't see an old anything—I just see a man. And two, you said you'd always be honest with me. It goes both ways, George. Why wouldn't you expect me to be honest with you? I always thought you were…" She cupped the side of his jaw, rubbing her palm against his morning beard stubble that was a handsome mosaic of tawny, dark brown and silver. What was the right word? *Distinguished? Powerful?* "…sexy."

He propped himself up on his elbow beside her, arching an eyebrow in doubt. "Explain."

She lifted her fingers to trace the eyebrow's curve. She traced the straight line of his nose and the square shape of his jaw before sliding across the impeccable sculpt of his lips. His hand slipped beneath her shirt again, settling at the nip of her waist while she explored each compelling angle.

"You're confident. Accomplished. So comfortable in your own skin. Do you have any idea how empowering, how hot it is to have a man like you interested in someone like me?"

"Someone like you?" His voice had dropped a note in pitch, grown husky.

Her gaze lowered to the placket of his shirt where she unhooked one button, then two, blazing a trail along skin that was rough, smooth, ticklish and always warm beneath her fingertips. "Anyone else would think I've gone nuts these past few days, but you keep saying you believe me."

"I do. I've seen the evidence of his cruelty."

"I'm complicated, George." She loosed another button and slipped her hand beneath the cotton to palm the firm plane of his chest and feel the muscles quiver beneath her touch. "I'm so worried about making mistakes and hurting someone I care about again that I stop relationships before they have a chance to begin." She inhaled his uniquely clean, masculine scent and got a whiff of something else that made her blush. "And I smell like dog shampoo this morning."

He laughed, catching her hand before she could pull it away, holding it against the taut male nipple and the beating heart underneath. "Maybe I think Eau de Spike is hot."

It was Elise's turn to laugh. She was shaking with the freedom of his honest humor, loving how the shared laughter eased the lines of stress on his face, when he dipped his head and stopped up her laughter with a kiss.

Instantly, the atmosphere in the room shifted. Humor gave way to hunger as Elise wound her arms around George's neck and he pulled her more firmly into the heat of his body. By heaven, did this man know how to kiss. Tenderly. Passionately. Seductively.

He wasn't bad with his hands, either. While

his lips roamed over her jaw and earlobe and temple, he unbuttoned the front of her paint shirt and spread it open on top of the quilt. His mouth followed the path of his fingers, touching, tasting, stroking, praising as his sandpapery beard tickled and his warm tongue soothed.

"You have such soft hair." He nuzzled her ear, pushed aside the worn collar and teased the sensitive bundle of nerves at the base of her throat. "These long legs? Let's just say I'm glad you like to wear dresses." He squeezed her bottom and drew his hand along her thigh as he kissed his way down to the curve of her breast. "You have miles of cool, creamy skin that I can't seem to stop touching."

"I won't stop you." Elise pushed his shirt off his shoulders, ran her fingers through his silky, sleep-rumpled hair, touched whatever she could reach. He was all hot, all muscle, all man.

He squeezed her breast and captured the beaded tip in his mouth, wetting the lace of her bra and making her ache to feel his tongue on her skin. "Don't tempt me."

Elise curled a leg around the back of his, pulling his weight partially on top of her. "Would this help?"

George lifted his head, squeezed his eyes shut and groaned before levering himself above her and rubbing his hard thigh against the seam of her shorts. She dug her fingers into his shoulders and held on as shock waves of desire rushed straight to her core at the feel of him there.

His eyes were dark with passion when they opened again. Every muscle in his body was rigid with the effort to retreat. "Ah, hell, Elise, I want to be inside you so badly I can't think straight."

She gradually found her voice again. "Then don't think. I want the same thing. It feels right."

He dropped a kiss on her tender lips. "Yeah, but, honey, I haven't done this for a while. I'm a little out of practice."

"Your parts all work, don't they?"

"Obviously." The pressure nudging between her thighs left no doubt of that. "But my style—"

"I don't need style, George. I need you." She worked the last buttons of his shirt free and found the snap of his jeans. His skin quivered beneath her hands as she gently unzipped him. "I need the man who always tells me the truth. The man I never have to doubt. Please. Just…"

"Just what?"

She paused with her hands at his hips, pushing his jeans and shorts out of her way. "Take me away from this nightmare for a while. Make me feel normal and healthy and brave."

"Brave?" He stroked her hair off her forehead.

"Brave enough to feel something and want someone—and not be afraid that there's a penalty attached to caring." She thought she'd feel a hesitation, an inner voice warning her to stop. But everything about this moment felt right. Everything about George felt right. "I need to know what it's like for a real, flesh and blood man to want me. Just for me. That is what you want, right?"

With a nod, he lowered his mouth to reclaim hers. "No hidden agenda. No conditions. Just you. I want you."

And then there was an eager bumping of hands and limbs as she helped George shuck his jeans and briefs, and he pulled her shorts and panties off to join them on the floor. He unhooked the front clasp of her bra and pushed it aside before squeezing and tonguing the sensitive tips into throbbing, tight beads. Elise mimicked the same exploration on him, loving the musky smell of his skin as she found each taut male nipple with her lips.

They were still half dressed on top when George pushed his hand down between her thighs and palmed the pressure building there. She bucked beneath the force of his hand, and bucked again when he slid two fingers inside to test her slick readiness for him.

"George," she gasped as she raised her knees and he settled himself between them. "Now."

He cursed against her breast, then kissed the spot. Apologized. "I don't have any protection."

She wrapped her legs around him, holding his hips in the cradle of hers when he would have pulled away. "I'm on the pill. Do you have any health issues?"

"No. You?"

"No." She caught his face between her hands and lifted her mouth to reclaim his. But he quickly took over the kiss, driving her back into the pillow, driving her weight into the bed, driving himself deeply inside her.

He held himself like that for several seconds while her body adjusted to welcome his, while her breasts pillowed beneath the weight of his chest, while her arms wound around him to hold him close.

"Are you good?" he whispered against her ear. She couldn't answer. She didn't want to talk. She just wanted to feel again. "Elise?"

She nodded, tightened her legs around his buttocks to open herself more fully and urged him even deeper. Who needed sexy words or seductive style when a man's desire for her was this straightforward, when he knew where to touch a woman. Where to kiss. What to… His fingers found that sensitive nub between them as he thrust inside her and she arched against him, gasping at the power of her release.

Elise soared to a place where the world made sense, where she was everything a woman should be, where the nightmare could no longer reach her, where she was safe, in George's arms.

When he drove into her one last time with a husky groan and found his own release, she knew, without a doubt, that she loved this man—that anything she'd once felt for Quinn Gallagher or Nikolai Titov or even James Westbrook was a pale comparison to the humbling emotions George Madigan had awakened inside her. This was the right man, the only man, for her.

They collapsed into each other's arms and dozed together, skin to skin, sated and whole, her energy spent, her spirit stronger than it had been for months. And yet, her future was still uncertain.

If only George wasn't the one man she couldn't have. Was she willing to lose the job that had given back her confidence and self-respect? Would George be willing to give her up at KCPD and let his office return to the slow-moving machine it had once been?

Did he even want the same things she wanted? Or was this blissful morning together a job perk for a man who would do his duty by her, but who wouldn't appreciate the complications of an ongoing commitment outside of the office? Apparently, there was still a lot more of *this* they needed to discuss.

But later. If she had a later.

She snuggled closer to the heat and strength of George's body, fearing this perfect morning might be the only one for them.

The alarm woke them a half hour later and the rest of the world demanded their attention again.

ELISE HAD TURNED on two lamps in her office, in addition to the overhead lights, to compensate for the turbulent gray clouds rolling in and blotting out the sun outside. With every bolt of lightning, the lights flickered. With every answering boom of thunder, she jumped inside her skin.

But as long as the power was on and her computer was working, she could finish typing the final draft of George's banquet speech while he was on the phone with Commissioner Cartwright-Masterson. The commissioner's daughter-in-law, Rebecca, had gone into labor during the night. With her son, Seth Cartwright, in the delivery room, and the rest of their extended family in the hospital waiting room, Rebecca had given birth to a daughter named Sydney.

Elise was glad for the numerous phone calls coming into the office, with meetings to reschedule, reporters to appease until an official statement could be issued, and friends and coworkers to update on the latest news from the top floors of KCPD headquarters. If she had any fewer calls to manage, any fewer reports to file, any fewer memos to send, she might have time to drive herself mad.

The worries that did creep in when her mind wandered could easily derail the normal routine she was clinging to this morning. She had an armed detective named Spencer Montgomery dog sitting Spike and watching her house for her. She'd fielded a call from Annie Fensom at the crime lab which hadn't offered much hope. They could approximate a shoe size on her stalker from the picture Nick had taken in her backyard. But unless they could compel every man in Kansas City with size twelve feet to give a DNA sample, there was still no way to identify the man who'd sent her those sick I-love-you messages.

The weather outside seemed to echo Elise's mood today. For a few wonderful minutes, she'd been happy and content in George's arms and the sun had been shining. But as the storm gathered force and the skies darkened at noon, her thoughts kept going back to all the reasons why she and George Madigan might never have more than this morning. First, there was the difference in their ages. She didn't think fourteen years was an issue, but it seemed to bother him. Then there was his position of authority over her. Her need to do the work she was so good at in order to prove her self-worth and redeem her past mistakes. Her scary track record with choosing the wrong men.

And if any of those obstacles weren't enough, she came with the extra baggage of a mysterious psychopath who said he loved her, but promised violence if she did anything he deemed a mistake.

Like making love with George and silently giving him her heart?

Those were probably two pretty unforgivable mistakes in the eyes of the man who would harm an innocent dog and terrorize a frightened woman.

The thunder shook and a new, terrifying thought turned Elise's gaze toward George's office door.

I don't want to hurt you or the things you love.

Would he hurt George? With every contact, the creep found new and more devious ways to terrorize her. He'd nearly broken her completely by making her think he'd attacked Spike. If he went after George or her parents or anyone else she cared about, she might never recover from the emotional destruction. How could she fight an enemy who preyed on her mind and emotions and refused to reveal his identity?

Lightning flashed in the bank of clouds overhead and thunder rattled the windows and furniture almost immediately. The tiny hairs on the back of her neck stood straight on end. Whatever new threat was coming was nearly on top of them.

The telephone rang and Elise let out a tiny yelp. Cursing her own skittishness, she inhaled a steadying breath and picked up the receiver. "Good morning, Deputy Commissioner Madigan's office. This is Elise."

"Good morning, Elise. Garrett Cho here."

"Deputy Commissioner Cho. How are you?" She eyed the greenish tinge of the squall line moving beneath the charcoal-gray cumulus clouds. "Hope you're battened down someplace safe. Looks like we're going to have a gully washer."

"At least. I don't think an umbrella will do us any good today." The deputy commissioner in charge of facilities management was always a friendly conversation. She smiled through the next thunderclap despite the tingling at her nape. Something about working in a high-rise building, that much closer to the root of a storm, always made it seem more intense. "I understand we're in for a temporary shuffle in command over the next few days. Commissioner Cartwright-Masterson's a grandmother?"

"Yes, sir. Deputy Commissioner Madigan is on the phone with her right now, going over the final details. She's taking a full week off to help her son and daughter-in-law adjust to being new parents."

Cho laughed. "We can run the department while she's gone. I'm not worried about that. And you can assure George that all of our precinct storm shelters are fully supplied and ready for whatever hits us today. But I'm more interested in the baby details. We had a pool going, you know."

Elise grinned as the second light on her phone went off. George's conversation with Commissioner Cartwright-Masterson had ended. She could transfer this call to him, but she knew he had plenty on his agenda already and decided to handle this social call herself. "Sydney Cartwright weighed in at seven pounds, fourteen ounces, and she arrived at 7:15 a.m. How'd you do?"

"Well, since I'd put my money on a baby boy—not very well. But as long as the mother and baby are fine, I shouldn't complain about losing five bucks." She could hear the teasing in Cho's voice. "Unless George won the pot. Then I'm complaining."

"I couldn't tell you that, sir. But I'll let him know you're thinking of him." A rock slammed into her high-rise window and she nearly jumped out of her chair. "What the…?"

Not a rock at all. A chunk of frozen rain. Dozens of hard, icy pellets hitting the windows. Hail.

"Elise?" Cho's tone was suddenly one of concern. "Are you all right?"

She steadied her breathing. "It's hailing here. The noise of it startled me, that's all."

"I'm north of town so the storm hasn't hit here yet." His voice grew as businesslike and commanding as she'd ever heard George's. "I'd better hang up and call my crew chiefs, make sure the facilities are all secure. People go nuts when the weather's bad. Thanks for the update."

Nuts. Yeah. Maybe the intense, unusual weather pattern was the reason her world had turned upside down this week.

"You bet. Goodbye, sir." George's door was open by the time she hung up.

"Anything important?" he asked, striding to her window to watch the hailstones collecting on the ledge outside. "Some of those are golf-ball-size. It must be pretty windy out there to keep sending the rain back up to the clouds."

Elise rose to stand beside him, although she seemed to jump every time one of those tiny missiles hit the window. "That was Garrett Cho—asking about Commissioner Cartwright-Masterson's granddaughter and assuring you his team is ready to deal with the storm and its aftermath."

"Good." The window fogged when he released a deep breath. With the subtlest of movements he reached across the few inches separating them and brushed the back of one finger along her arm up to her shoulder. "Goose bumps. From the storm or something else?"

He might hurt the things you care about.

As much as she wanted to turn into that

caress, she knew it was wiser to cross her arms and pull away. "We really shouldn't. Not here."

The gruffness returned to his tone. "You didn't answer my question."

And she wouldn't get a chance to. Her phone rang and Elise returned to her desk. Recognizing the line that lit up, she answered. "Hey, Shane. What's going on?"

"Hey, Elise—I mean, Miss Brown—um, there's a James Westbrook heading to your office. He doesn't have an appointment, but he told me he's here to see you, not the deputy commissioner. He said he's a friend, so is that okay?"

"He's coming here? Now?"

Not the reaction Shane had expected. She heard his chair bang against the wall or desk as he stood too quickly. "Do you need me to come get him?"

And do what, arrest him? She didn't even know what James wanted yet. Just because she didn't want to deal with another confrontation didn't justify sending an armed police officer after him. "No. I just have other things I need to do this morning. Thanks, Shane, I'll handle it."

There was a sharp rap at the door before she hung up the phone. When she saw James's dripping clothes and fogged-up glasses, her *What do you want?* became "You're soaking wet." Elise grabbed the box of tissues on her desk and hurried across the room, pulling out several to hand to him when he tried to wipe off his glasses on his sopping oxford shirt. "Here."

"I could have swum across the street from the parking garage." He wiped his face with more tissues before putting his glasses back on and pointing to the window. "Man, it's a bear driving out there. I could barely see beyond my headlights."

Elise glanced over her shoulder, meeting George's inquisitive glare before looking past him. The hail had stopped as quickly as it had started, leaving what looked like snowfall outside on the ledge. But the wind gusted a wave of rain against the glass, washing away her view.

Ignoring both Mother Nature and the sturdy forearms crossed over George's chest, Elise urged James to the sofa before crossing to a storage closet. "I've got a stash of hand towels here. Have a seat. The leather's been waterproofed."

She wasn't foolish enough to think James had come here to discuss the weather. But she wasn't prepared for his anger to follow her across the room. "I want to know why the police stopped by my apartment and called my father to find out if we had proof that we were at the ball game yesterday afternoon. Proof! Can you imagine the questions Dad was asking me? That pesky little detective said he was even going to find out who was selling frosty malts in our section at the stadium to see if the guy remembered seeing me there."

George moved several steps closer, inviting himself into the one-sided conversation. "What did you tell Detective Fensom?"

"Why did Detective Fensom ask?" For a moment, James lost interest in Elise and drying off. Instead, he went toe-to-toe with George, dripping on the rug in front of him. "This is about me interrupting your little date the other night, isn't it. You're abusing your power, Madigan. If you're trying to force me out of Elise's life, it won't work."

"What did you tell Detective Fensom?"

James snatched the towel Elise handed him and pulled off his glasses to wipe his face and hair. "I was at the game. The Royals won. My father will tell you the same thing, and so will the guy who sold me the frosty malts."

George wasn't fazed by James's accusation or the puddle on his carpet. "And you didn't leave the stadium at all."

Shoving his fingers through his hair to comb the blond spikes back into order, James refused to answer. "I'm beginning to think that you've been lying to me, Lise.

"Lying? How?"

"You don't want to be friends. You put your boyfriend up to this harassment campaign."

"George isn't my boy—"

"I don't think you want to see me at all."

Not when he was like this. He'd never been this petulant and temperamental back in college. She never would have gone out with him if he had been. But three years of dating and almost marrying a man made him deserving of some type of explanation. "There was another incident yesterday, James. The deputy commissioner and Detective Fensom are investigating. Someone tried to…frighten me."

"Someone tried to kidnap her," George corrected, driving home the reason for his so-called harassment. A boom of thunder punctuated the danger she'd faced, and Elise shivered. He pointed to her sandals and the purple bruise and bandages on her right foot. "Someone assaulted her."

Pretty minor injury compared to the damage done to her peace of mind and any sense of security she'd once had.

"And you think it was me?" James turned his narrowed eyes on her. "That's rich." He paced to the door, then came back, pointing an accusing finger at them both. "This is just like that investigation in Europe. Having to prove my innocence when I wasn't guilty of a damn thing."

George kept pushing for answers. "The death of your girlfriend?"

"Oh, so you checked that out, too. That's why that cop out by the elevator frisked me before I could come see you." She wondered if it was grief that made him look so suddenly gray and gaunt. "Because you think I'm going to kill you, too?"

"James!" Elise's knees wobbled and she quickly sat in the closest chair. Whether fueled by anger or grief, his words cut her to the quick. She hadn't believed the man she'd once loved would want to hurt her. But she hadn't known just how much pain he'd been in, either.

George took a step toward James, forcing him to retreat without ever touching him. "Officer Wilkins was doing his job, Westbrook. We're on heightened security this week. Even if you had an appointment, he wouldn't let you just wander in here. And I'm guessing you don't have an appointment."

"I came to see Elise. Not you."

"Unless you start talking to her with some respect, you're going to be dealing with me."

James seemed to consider George's threat. Maybe he hadn't realized how vile his words had sounded. If he'd been lashing out in grief, she could forgive that. But George wasn't about to.

"You leave now and deal with my detectives," he warned, "or you answer our questions."

Making his decision, James sank onto the couch opposite Elise. "I'm sorry, Lise. You know I didn't mean that. I love you."

Not the most comforting words a volatile man could say to her right now. "You loved your girlfriend."

"My fiancée," he corrected, conveying the depth of his grief. James wadded the towel in his hands, then shook it out and folded it neatly before saying anything more. "Marta's death was an accident. Our car went off the road and hit a bridge abutment. I survived with barely a scratch because I had my seat belt on. But she didn't even make it to the ambulance."

How awful. If he'd loved Marta as much as he claimed, it was no wonder he'd taken a leave from his job and come home to Kansas City. Home was almost always the best place to heal a wound like that. "I'm so sorry."

George sat on the arm of her chair and rested his hand on her shoulder, gently halting her from saying anything more. "Was there an inquiry?"

James nodded, his normally bright eyes looking dull and sad. "I couldn't even grieve, there were too many cops asking too many questions. Accusing me of things like staging the accident. I think if I'd died, too, they wouldn't have cared."

"Don't say that."

"You're probably thinking that I want to replace Marta with you. I don't. I know you and I were done a long time ago. But until I find someone else and can move on, I thought it'd be nice to have a friend."

She blinked back the tears that stung her eyes. Could grief and anger twist a man's psyche until he couldn't distinguish reality from the relationship he'd lost? Was James the threat George suspected him to be? A familiar face and playing on her sympathies would make a perfect disguise for a man who wanted to divert suspicion from himself.

"It's okay, Lise." James leaned forward, stretching out his hand to hers, perhaps misreading her silent tears. But she couldn't seem to make herself reach out to clasp the peace offering. "I want you to know I was cleared of any charges. You don't have to be afraid of me." Maybe he hadn't misread her at all. His gaze shifted up to George. "And your cop friend here doesn't need to sic his buddies on me, either."

The whole building vibrated with a low-pitched drum roll of thunder that lasted several seconds. And maybe it was just Elise's imagination, but the building seemed to be swaying with the wind. "Has anyone checked the weather report lately?"

James straightened. His blue eyes flickered over her, perhaps gauging her concern, perhaps judging her for refusing to take his hand. "Something bad's coming. You feel it, too, don't you."

Elise shivered. The barometric pressure must have suddenly dropped. "I was hoping for something a little more scientific."

George patted her shoulder and nodded to her desk. "Why don't you get online—see if there are any new watches or warnings we need to be aware of. I'll show Mr. Westbrook out."

She nodded and got up, relieved to have something to do besides sit there and wonder what James's hand would feel like in a leather glove against her skin. Would there be a shock of recognition to the man on the Plaza?

"Goodbye, Lise," James called after her.

She didn't even care that he still had the damp towel draped around his neck. Until she was certain of his innocence—of any man's innocence or guilt—she couldn't afford to be too trusting or forgiving, or care too much that an old friend was hurting. "Bye, James."

Pulling up the local weather, she cringed at the swath of dark red and orange that covered a good portion of the state line—including almost all of Kansas City.

When George strolled back in, he was rolling up the sleeves of his blue shirt. "The guy tells a good story."

Elise glanced up. "Do you think James was making that up about his fiancée? He seemed so heartbroken."

"It'd be a good way to gain your sympathy and trust, which is exactly what the sleazeball who's trying to get his hands on you would do." He arched a dark eyebrow. "You weren't completely buying it, either. You wouldn't touch him."

George had noticed. That meant James had probably noticed the slight, too. "I kept thinking of the man who grabbed me on the Plaza. What if his grip felt the same?"

"All the more reason to shoo him out of here." He loosened his tie and unbuttoned his collar next, a sure sign the man was getting down to some serious work. "I told Shane to escort him all the way downstairs and keep an eye on him until he leaves the building. The kid's eager to do me a favor and get a good recommendation for making detective. Westbrook can wait in the lobby until the storm lets up."

"And if that story's legit and James's grief is real?"

"Then it upset you. And I don't like that, either."

As much as she loved having George stand up to protect her, she could already see how letting their personal feelings into their working relationship was compromising their professionalism. "You're the face of KCPD now, while the commissioner is gone. You can't put me above—"

The lights in the room blinked off and on, a sure sign the weather was getting worse. Her argument died on her lips and she stood. The windows rattled beneath another assault of wind.

"That's not good." George moved to the window, peering out into the wall of rain and darkness there. "What have we got?"

Although Elise's computer had shut down and was busy powering up again, she'd memorized the dangers swirling around them. "Thunderstorm warnings. Strong winds. Heavy rain. Several tornado watches in the area."

He drummed his fingers against the windowsill.

"What are you thinking?" Elise asked.

"An ounce of prevention…" He brought his hand back to his gun and badge at his waist. Decision made, he faced her. "We need to move downstairs. Find out how many people are on the top floors and let's send out a text and call advisory."

The boss was back. This, she knew how to handle. "Right."

She sat down at her computer and pulled up the program to issue a building-wide text and phone alert. She was pulling up a separate screen to get a list of personnel checked in on the top three floors when she heard wet shoes squeaking on the hallway's marble floor.

Elise glanced up. "Shane's not at his post to screen visitors."

George warned her to stay put at her desk. With his hand on the butt of his gun, he moved toward the open door. "Keep working. I'll check it out. Ah, hell."

Courtney Reiter came through the doorway with her arms wide-open, and wrapped them around George. "Thank God I got here in one piece."

With Courtney's wet hair and dripping yellow trench coat soaking his clothes, George took her by the shoulders and gently pushed her away. "This is not a good time, Court."

The normally stunning blonde looked almost waifish as she clung to her ex-husband's wrists. From this distance, Elise couldn't tell if it was the rain or tears that left the other woman's mascara running in rivulets down each cheek. "I could have been trapped in that elevator when the power went out. Do you have any idea how frightening that is? You know how scared I am of storms."

"What are you doing here?" With a glance over Courtney's head and a nod toward the closet, he instructed Elise to find them more towels.

"Where were you last night, George?" the blonde accused. "And don't say working because I called here as well as your cell number and you never answered. I left messages and you never called me back. Did you see all that rain we had?"

"I was aware of the storm." He draped an arm around her shoulders and led her to the hallway. "We're in the middle of dealing with round two right now, so I'm going to ask you to leave. You can wait downstairs where it's safe until the storm passes."

The woman might appear helpless, but she was definitely persistent. With a quick turn, she spun free of George's grasp and walked over to the sitting area. "The ground was so dry that the rain leaked right into the basement of our house."

"Your house, Court—"

"It's probably ankle deep by now." She sat, nodding her thanks when Elise handed her a towel. And she kept right on talking as Elise gave George a towel to dab at his sleeves and shirtfront. "I had a creek running from one of those egress windows right through to the laundry room drain. I had to move all my storage boxes up onto shelves and two-by-fours. I needed your help and you weren't…" Elise's hands must have lingered too long on the towel George pressed against his shoulder. She turned to see Courtney staring right at her. "You were with her, weren't you?"

Elise felt the stillness come over George's body and recognized the quiet anger in him. Putting the towel in Elise's hands, he nudged her toward her desk. "Get that alert sent out. Now."

"Oh, my God." Courtney smeared mascara

across her cheek as she blotted her face with the towel. "I knew there was something going on between the two of you. Isn't an affair with your secretary against departmental regulations?"

George took Courtney by the arm and pulled her to her feet. "Let it go. You and I aren't married anymore."

Smarting at the barb aimed squarely at her, Elise clicked Send, relaying the deputy commissioner's order to close down shop and head for lower floors in the HQ building. "Message sent, sir."

An accusation like George's ex had made was exactly the sort of thing that could cost Elise her job, and make it difficult to get hired on someplace else. And, being labeled the woman who ignored the rules and slept with her boss wouldn't do a whole lot for the personal reputation she'd worked so hard to rebuild.

"Good. Now make sure we've got our key files backed up and shut things down so we can head down, too."

This time, Courtney couldn't extricate herself from George's firmer grasp. "In my head, I always knew you'd move on one day. But then, for so long, you never did. I guess I took it for granted that you and I... I made such a mistake when I left you, didn't I."

After tipping his head back in a frustrated sigh, George turned the curvy blonde to face him. "We're ancient history, Court. I will always care about you, but I am never going to be in love with you again."

"Are you in love with her?"

Elise froze at her desk, hugging a stack of files to her chest and waiting far too expectantly for George's answer. Did he love her? Even this morning, when they'd been so close and had shared so much, he'd never said the words.

Her heart plummeted to her stomach. He didn't say them now.

"I can't be at your beck and call whenever you need something, Court. I'm tired of feeling guilty about not being there for you when I was starting my career and working the streets. There's only so much penance a man can pay." He turned her toward the door. "Now go. Be a grown-up. You need to learn to face your problems. I've got my own to deal with."

When George walked back to his office, Courtney followed. "This isn't fair, you know. You're an executive now. You work at a desk. You go home every night." She pointed to Elise who quickly went back to gathering files and shutting down the computer. "She doesn't have to worry about whether or not you're coming home at all, the way I did. It isn't fair."

"I'm the same man, Courtney." George stopped in the doorway to his office and turned, plucking his badge from his belt and holding it up. "I'm still a cop. We'll never fit." His gaze drifted across the room to find Elise. He repeated the same phrase, his quieter tone turning it into some kind of vow, some kind of promise, to her. "I'm a cop."

Elise narrowed her gaze, questioning the message he was sending.

But before he explained, before she understood, he snapped his badge back into place and offered Courtney a rueful smile. "You didn't want a cop then. And you don't want one now. You wanted an executive. I've got the trappings now, but it's not me. Underneath the suit and tie, I'm still just a cop."

"No, you're—" Whatever Courtney was about to say ended with a startled shriek.

The tornado sirens went off.

Chapter Ten

A clap of thunder exploded overhead, shaking the building so badly, it felt as if a bomb had gone off. It knocked over Spike's picture on her desk and Elise gripped the back of her chair. Courtney screamed and covered her ears, collapsing into the door frame beside George. "It's so loud. I can't stand it when it's so loud."

"We need to get to the storm shelter!" George shouted above the wail of the sirens. "Emergency procedure alpha, now!"

Elise nodded. She pulled her purse from the bottom drawer of her desk and dropped Spike's picture inside. Then she opened the center drawer to retrieve her emergency two-way radio and a bracelet full of keys she slipped onto her wrist.

George took Courtney by the shoulders and pulled her to her feet. "Take the stairs all the way to the basement, Court. The men's and women's locker rooms, firing range and workout facilities are down there. Someone will show you where to go. You'll be safe."

Courtney latched on as soon as George let go. "You're not coming?"

He looked over Courtney's shoulder to Elise. "You've got your building access keys?"

Raising her arm, Elise jangled her wrist. She looped her bag over her shoulder and picked up the phone to dial the prearranged number to Cliff Brandt at the utilities office. "Everything on our hard drives is backed up to remote servers. Do you want me to put the flash drives in my purse and take them with me?"

"Negative." George left his ex-wife leaning against the wall and ran into his office to retrieve his own radio and a flashlight. When he came back he was tucking his cell phone into his pocket. "One of those lightning strikes must have taken out the cell tower on the roof. I've got no reception."

Courtney whimpered as a flash of lightning lit up the sky and the thunder retaliated with another boom. Elise put the phone on speaker mode as the utilities director answered.

"Cliff?" George leaned over her desk to speak. "I need to know if we've got any blackout areas." They both turned to the pounding of footsteps in the marble hallway. Other staff heading for shelter? George thumbed over his shoulder, urging her to join them, and returned to his call. "If there are sections of the city without televisions or working sirens, I want to dispatch units to get people to shelter immediately."

"Sir?" Shane Wilkins appeared in the doorway from the hall, his chest heaving with deep breaths. When he spotted George and Elise, he jogged into the room. "We've got to get out of here. Doppler radar spotted a rotating storm cell south of here. Heading northeast. Right for the city. Spotters on the ground already reported a funnel cloud touching down on the Kansas side of the river."

George straightened. "What the hell are you doing up here? Did Westbrook go out in this? I want to keep eyes on that guy."

Shane turned to Elise, as if his superior officer hadn't understood the urgency of his announcement. "Look, I ran up here to let you guys know. The elevators are shut down already. We're right in the storm's path. The tornado is coming here. Downtown K.C."

"You ran up eight flights of stairs?" Elise asked, astounded by the effort he'd made to warn them.

The uniformed officer nodded. His nostrils flared as he regained control of his breathing after his wind sprint. "Cell reception is spotty. Except for Dispatch, landlines are for outgoing or station-to-station calls only during an emergency, not personal calls within the building. You guys are my responsibility. I volunteered."

Elise smiled her thanks for his dedication to his duty and squeezed his arm. "You're one in a million, Shane."

George jotted down the information he needed and ended his call. He tore off the note and handed it to Elise. "Go. Get on your radio to Dispatch and tell them to send a unit to these areas. Tell them no heroics, on my command. The officers make the announcement, then get to shelter themselves. That goes for you, too." He grabbed Elise's hand, giving it a subtle squeeze as he pulled her toward the door and released her. She stopped. He wasn't coming with her? No, he was looking up at the blond-haired officer. "Wilkins?"

"Sir." Shane snapped to attention.

George poked the center of his flak vest. "No. Heroics. I'm not planning on losing any of my men today." He held up his own radio. "You should have used one of these instead of running up here."

"Oh. Right." The younger man's shoulders

sagged. "I knew that. I guess I just wanted to see for myself that you all were okay."

"You're too young to know you're not invincible yet." Shaking his head, George tucked his radio onto his belt and pocketed his flashlight. "But I do need you to do something for me."

"Sir?" Shane's dull green eyes brightened with the chance to redeem himself in his commanding officer's eyes.

"I want you to do a room-to-room search up here to make sure the entire floor is evacuated. Radio the guards on each level to do the same and get everyone to the basement ASAP. Including yourselves. And remember, this is no drill. Be thorough, but be fast."

"I'm on it." Striding past Elise, Shane turned his mouth to the radio on his shoulder, relaying George's order.

George nearly ran into Elise when he turned back to his office. His look included both her and Courtney. "What are you two still doing here? I gave you an order."

Her worries about departmental regulations and forbidden relationships didn't seem important right now. She splayed her hand on the left side of his chest, seeking out the familiar, strong beat of his heart. "Why aren't you leaving? He said the storm was heading right for us."

George covered her hand with his, sealing this powerful connection between them. "I'm a cop, remember? And with the commissioner off the clock, I'm the one in charge. I'm going to back up Shane. Make sure all the floors are clear. Time is of the essence." Without a moment's hesitation, he leaned in and captured her mouth in a kiss. It was sweet and urgent and perfect. He raised his lips to her forehead and kissed her again before releasing her. "Don't worry. I'll meet you in the basement."

"You'd better." She curled her fingers around his tie, holding on a moment longer. "Or else, I'll come looking for you."

"Always keeping me on task, aren't you." He smiled and gave her one more hard, quick kiss, before hurrying past her out the door. "Wilkins!" he called out. "Give me your twenty." He disappeared to the left and was gone.

"You really do love him, don't you?"

Elise turned to the blonde woman. Courtney was a pale shadow of her usual beauty, with her dark gaze leaping to the window at every gust of wind. But even though her observation was on target, Elise's feelings were too fragile, maybe even too futile to admit to anyone.

"George is counting on us to do our job, Ms. Reiter, so he can do his." Although she imagined that hers was not the help Courtney wanted, Elise crossed the room and linked their arms together, pulling the woman into step beside her. "Come on. We have to get out of here."

Coaxing the frightened woman along every step of the way, Elise hurried as fast as they could to the stairwell beside the elevator. She radioed the information George requested to Dispatch and tucked her radio into her purse. With every flight of stairs, they joined more officers, visitors, administrators and support staff on their way down to the basement. With every floor they descended, the concussive noise of the wind and rain and the scream of the warning siren faded.

Elise led Courtney down the last flight of stairs into a crowded hallway where a uniformed officer directed them into the men's locker room. Another officer there told them to find a seat against the concrete block wall near the showers.

"All these people work here?" Courtney seemed to be realizing for the first time just how many dedicated men and women worked for the police department.

"Most of them." Elise helped the other woman off with her yellow coat. While Courtney folded it up to make a cushion for herself on the concrete floor, Elise stretched up on tiptoe to scan all the faces for any sign that George had made it safely down to the shelter with them. There were a lot of people crowding into the rooms down here. "This is just the headquarters and Fourth Precinct building. Each of the precincts employs almost as many people."

"And George is in charge of all of them?"

"Until Commissioner Cartwright-Masterson comes back to work, yes." Was Courtney just now beginning to understand the responsibilities her ex-husband carried on his shoulders? Could she comprehend that he needed a partner who could be a help to him, and not a drain on his time and emotional energy? "Do you see him anywhere?"

Instead of finding that distinguished dark hair spattered with silver, she spotted a familiar head of blond hair slicked back with water—and the beige towel from her office draped around the man's neck. Elise climbed over a bench to reach him before he turned the corner. "James?"

"Lise." He stepped out of the line he'd been following and excused his way back to her.

"I thought you'd left." She hated the feeling crawling up her skin when a group she recognized from the tech squad jostled past her. Despite their apologies and a forgiving smile from her, she was developing a serious phobia about crowds of people.

"Here." James helped her get back across the bench and out of the flow of human traffic. "The siren went off before I could get to my car. An officer in the lobby instructed me to come down here."

"You mean Officer Wilkins."

"I didn't catch her name." Her? Definitely not Shane. "You mean the tall guy who escorted me out? He ran off like he had a mission of some kind."

Elise felt a tug at the hem of her dress. "Who's your friend, Elise?"

"Oh, this is Courtney Reiter. This is—" she hoped this could still be the truth "—my friend. James Westbrook."

When they shook hands, Courtney held on to pull herself up. "Nice to meet you."

James nodded. "Pleasure."

"Are you a police officer?"

He shook his head. "Financial consultant."

"Really?" Did Elise imagine the healthy color that seeped into Courtney's face? "No gun? No badge?"

"No." He released Courtney's hand and turned to Elise. "Look, I'm sorry about what happened upstairs. I guess I'm a bigger mess than I realized. I lost Marta, I left my job. I know you're going through something now and you needed me to be there and I wasn't—"

"Let's not talk about that now." She glanced around the room at all the anxious faces. The building was rattling above their heads. The sirens were still sounding their warning. "We have bigger things to worry about right now."

"May I have your attention, please! Everyone!" A black man with streaks of gray in his hair and a badge hanging around his neck shouted above the noise in the room. Elise recognized Joe Hendricks, the fourth precinct watch commander—probably the highest ranking officer in the room. Instantly, the conversations fell silent and people stopped moving to listen. "We've been keeping up on the latest weather updates. At this time, I need everyone to have a seat against the wall. If your back's not against a concrete block. Find one."

The three of them sat on the floor while Captain Hendricks gave more orders regarding radio silence except for certain officers, and head counts for staff and guests. With Courtney wedged in the middle, Elise scooted closer, allowing as much room as possible to accommodate everyone taking shelter here.

Without a roomful of voices echoing off the

concrete walls, Elise could hear the wind raging above them. She wondered what kind of devastation was raining down on the city. And she worried that George was still upstairs somewhere, facing the storm head-on. And then... silence.

Elise's breath caught in her chest. Everyone in the room seemed to be looking upward, holding their breaths.

Sitting shoulder to shoulder, she felt Courtney shivering beside her. "Why is it so quiet?"

Elise hugged her purse to her chest, warding off the dreadful anticipation that twisted her stomach into knots. "The rain stopped."

Courtney raised her voice above a whisper. "That's good, right? Now they'll turn off that horrid siren."

Elise shushed her. "No. That silence is very bad."

James nudged Courtney's shoulder with his, trying to cajole her out of her fears. "The tornado is close enough to suck up all the rain. I remember a storm like this when I was a kid growing up east of here."

"Really?" Courtney turned her attention to James. "You've survived one of these before?"

"Yeah."

"Could I...?" She looped her arm through

James's and leaned against him. "Could I hold on to you? I'm afraid of storms."

"Sure." When James looked over Courtney's head, Elise shrugged.

Why not? It wasn't as if this wasn't already the strangest week of her life. James needed a new project to focus on—and Courtney Reiter was definitely a project. It was almost a relief to see him put his arm around Courtney's shoulder and hug her to his side.

"We'll be fine down here," he assured her. "All these reinforced walls? Below ground level? We'll be safe."

Not all of them were safe.

"Captain Hendricks said to do an office roll call, right?" She really didn't need anyone to answer. "We're all here. Where's George?"

I'll meet you in the basement.

You'd better. Or else, I'll come looking for you.

Something wasn't right. As surely as she had known an intruder had violated her bedroom, a man had followed her into a restroom during a blackout and that any of a dozen different weird events had been real threats and not tricks of her imagination, she knew that George was in trouble. It was her job to take care of him, just as he'd made it his job to protect her.

"Will you look after Courtney, James? Make sure she stays safe?" She slid the bracelet of keys up her arm, tucked the radio into her pocket and pushed herself up the wall to her feet.

He nodded. "Where are you going?"

She dropped her purse in her spot so she could move quickly through the room without hitting anyone. "To the other locker room. George isn't in here. I need to make sure he's safe."

Perhaps a sharp-eyed wariness or determined purpose to her movements made others lean back or pull their feet out of her path as she stayed as low to the floor as she could while stepping over the bench and circling around several banks of lockers. But every "Excuse me" she uttered, every nod she traded, put her no closer to spying any sign of a damp blue shirt or that salt-and-pepper hair.

She'd nearly reached the exit when a concerned voice called out to her. "Elise? You need to sit down."

Recognizing the uniformed officer, she squatted down beside him. "Officer Hale. Have you seen the deputy commissioner?"

"No, ma'am."

His dark hair was wet, his shirt plastered to the flak vest he wore underneath. "How bad is it out there?"

"Bad. Nobody needs to be outside right now."

Or on the upper floors of this building. "Could you try to get him on your radio? I don't want to interfere with emergency transmissions."

With a nod from Joe Hendricks, Denton turned his mouth to his shoulder and turned on his radio. "Commissioner Madigan, what's your twenty? This is Officer Hale, badge number 1897." Static was the only reply. "Commissioner Madigan, do you copy?"

"Why doesn't he answer?"

"He could be on a different frequency. His battery's dead. He's taken shelter behind a wall that blocks his signal. Lots of reasons."

She looked to Captain Hendricks for permission, as well. "May I?"

"Do it."

Elise pulled out her portable radio. "George? This is Elise. Where are you? You said no heroics, remember?" The answering static squealed—probably from a lightning strike disrupting the electricity in the air. "Just let me know you're safe."

Still no answer. Fear squeezed her heart.

"Something's not right." She pocketed her radio and stood again. "I'm going to the ladies' locker room and the firing range to look for him."

But her ears popped with a sudden change in air pressure. She braced her hand on the wall for balance and felt the subtle vibrations in the steel-and-concrete structure. She was too late.

The roar of a freight train hit the building above their heads.

"Get down, Elise!" Joe Hendricks ordered.

Officer Hale grabbed Elise's wrist and pulled her to the floor beside him as they heard explosions of glass and flying debris overhead. "Your search for loverboy will have to wait."

Denton Hale was wearing a black leather glove.

She flashed back to the Plaza and the gloved hand that had yanked her through the crowd. Her panic was instant and terrifying. She jerked her arm from his grasp and scooted across the aisle to sit next to Joe, despite the curious frown on Hale's face. At least with the captain as a buffer between them, she wouldn't have to worry about Hale being able to hurt her.

"Oh, my God," she whispered. She swept her gaze around the room. Every single uniformed police officer in this room was either wearing gloves, or had them tucked into their utility belts.

Loverboy? Surely that snide nickname meant

he was the only cop in this room she had to worry about.

She hugged her legs to her chest and kept Denton Hale in her sight for as long as possible, until the watch commander ordered them all to cover their heads.

The tornado was here.

GEORGE OPENED THE fifth-floor men's room and ran a sweep with his flashlight.

Three floors cleared.

Four minutes time.

Five persons routed from various rooms and sent down to the sublevel storm shelter.

He listened to the chatter on his radio as officers on each floor reported in and then got themselves downstairs. He and Shane were the last ones through each floor, running a quick secondary sweep. Although the back of his mind was filled with thoughts of Elise and visions that she'd made it safely to the basement without Courtney getting on her nerves or any other incident stopping her, he made himself focus on the job at hand. He couldn't be prouder of his department and the way the men and women who served under him were handling one weather-related crisis after another this summer.

And he couldn't be more anxious to confess the stunning revelation he'd made about himself, his work and his relationships upstairs in his office before the sirens had gone off to Elise. If he didn't get the chance to tell that woman how much he loved her and everything he was willing to do for them to be together, then he and Mother Nature were going to have words.

But he had a duty to this department and the entire city he needed to complete first before he could grab a little happiness for himself.

"Clear!" He moved next door to the ladies' room, but had taken only a couple of steps inside when the air pressure around him plummeted and his ears were suddenly stopped up with pain. "Ahh."

Not good.

He checked his watch. Five minutes had elapsed.

"Anybody in here?" He swallowed and yawned until his ears popped, and then he was suddenly aware of the eerie silence, broken only by the blare of the storm sirens.

Really not good.

Search time was over.

George pulled his radio from his belt. "Wilkins! Wherever you are, get to the basement now! If there's anyone left up here, they're on their own."

Fortunately, George was on the right side of the door when the row of tiny windows at the end of the stalls exploded into the room. The force of the blast threw him to the floor of the hallway. He hit hard and skidded across the floor as shards of glass pelted the marble tiles behind him like hail stones.

"Ah, hell." The roar of the wind was deafening, like a locomotive crashing at full speed into the side of the mountain. George pulled himself up onto his bruised knees and stood. A trash can beside the water fountain hovered off the floor, then flew past him and smashed into the wall. This wasn't any child's storybook with houses and dogs dropping into a colorful land.

This tornado was real.

And he was far too close to the heart of it.

"Wilkins!" That kid had better already be two steps ahead of him. George ran toward the double walls and steel doors of the stairwell, but his forward progress was more like fighting to escape the gravity of a black hole.

And then he heard the glass breaking inside the last office on his right. "Wilkins?"

The cry of pain he heard wasn't the storm and it wasn't his imagination.

"Shane!" George pushed open the door and immediately ducked his head as books and papers and a barrage of knickknacks got sucked out of the room. His tie whipped him in the face and the wind itself made it hard to open his eyes more than a squint. "Shane, are you in here? Are you injured?"

Grabbing the edge of a built-in bookshelf, George pulled himself along the front wall of the room. He was pelted with more books and debris before he reached a heavy office desk and dropped down beside it. The sturdy walnut shifted a little on the carpet, but blocked enough of the wind and flying missiles to allow him to search most of the room. "Wilkins?"

Following the sound of another moan, he crawled around the desk. Still no sign of the other officer. But his knee crunched down on a broken piece of glass, drawing his attention to the window above him.

George scanned the carpet around him and frowned. "One piece of glass?"

The floor in the bathroom had been littered with thousands. Holding tight to the desk, George pulled himself up and threw himself toward the shattered window. Bits of dirt stung his face like shrapnel, but he pushed his back against the wall and opened one eye to peer outside. He could see the funnel cloud coming up the street, more a giant cloud of flying dirt and debris than the spinning corkscrew he'd imagined. It picked up a car and dashed it against a streetlamp, bending the steel in half and shooting up sparks of electricity that were quickly swallowed by the storm.

Most important, he saw all the bits of glass wedged beneath the window frame and stuck into the concrete ledge outside the window.

George braced his forearm over his eyes and turned to verify the horrible suspicion burning in his gut. This wasn't Mother Nature's handiwork. Someone had deliberately broken this window.

He glimpsed a blur of blue from the corner of his eye, but it was too late to react. Something hard whacked him on the back of his head and neck, driving him to his knees. Another blow dropped him to the carpet, and in his spinning vision he saw the metal chair being thrown across the room. Probably what the perp had smashed the window with.

It had all been a trick, a perfectly plausible ruse to lure him into the room, to trap him here. Maybe even to kill him. And no one would suspect anything other than the tornado had been responsible. *Smart boy. I always knew you could accomplish anything you set your mind to.*

"You stay away from her. Elise is mine."

With the wind knocked from his lungs and his head spinning, George was too weak to stop Shane Wilkins from stealing his keys, radio and gun, and throwing them out the window.

The wind was roaring louder than his thoughts as Shane locked the door behind him, leaving George with no way to get down to the storm shelter now.

But George was a smart man, too. He rolled underneath the heavy desk as the tornado hit the building and thanked God that he was conscious and able to think.

Now he just had to live. Or else, Elise wouldn't.

Chapter Eleven

The moment the sirens stopped and Joe Hendricks gave the all clear, Elise pushed her way out of the ladies' locker room and moved upstream against a sea of people spilling out into the hallway and heading toward the stairs to assess damage and to find daylight and working phones to call loved ones.

"George?" Her worried shout was swallowed up by the mass of bodies. But, desperate to find him, to know he was okay, she shoved her way into the men's locker room to look for him. In here there were people with cuts and concussions being tended by the medics on staff and a nurse who'd been meeting her husband for lunch in the building. Careful to stay out of everyone's way as she searched, she stepped up onto the long bench between two rows of lockers and called again. "Is Deputy Commissioner Madigan in here?"

There were several nos and "I haven't seen

hims," but no replies that could give her the information she needed.

The crowd of survivors was thinning out when she went across the hall to check the firing range. One woman said she'd met the deputy commissioner on the stairs, going onto the sixth floor. He'd warned her to get downstairs fast and had promised to join them once the tornado got close enough to keep him from safely clearing all the floors.

But no George. She had a sick, sick feeling that something terrible had happened. That her gun-shy caution about relationships and fears of becoming a detriment to George's office if she gave in to her emotions had prevented her from telling him the truth. She should have been braver. She should have taken the risk and told him how much she loved him.

"Where are you?" she whispered, finally joining the flow of people to get back to her purse in the ladies' locker room.

Captain Hendricks had turned this space into an impromptu command center, deploying officers to various parts of the building to check for damage, sending others on out to neighborhoods and hospitals in the area to assist and protect emergency teams there. He was being briefed by other officers and approving a statement for the press liaison. There were reports of extensive property damage already coming in, threats of flash flooding near the river and the creeks and sloughs that fed into it, hail damage and more. Everyone had a job or was awaiting an order.

No one was looking for the man in charge of it all.

"Have you found him yet?"

Elise jumped at the hand on her elbow and jerked away from Denton Hale's touch. She supposed that coming right out and accusing him of being her stalker wouldn't be the smartest move, even surrounded by a roomful of policemen and women. Better to stay friendly and act as if she didn't suspect a thing. "No. Not yet."

Denton tapped the radio on his shoulder. "I tried to hail him a couple more times once the captain gave us the all clear. Sorry, though, I'm still getting nothing but static."

She forced a smile onto her lips. "Thank you for checking."

A distant drum of thunder reminded her that the storm hadn't finished yet. But the sound of rain hitting the ground and windows upstairs was a much gentler threat, maybe even a cleansing aftermath to the tornado's fury.

But the threat was still here, standing much

closer than any lightning bolt or rain cloud outside. "Do you want me to go with you to help look for him?" Officer Hale asked.

"No." She answered a little too quickly. When his eyes narrowed and looked at her like she was a crazy lady, Elise came up with another smile. "No, thank you." When Joe Hendricks called Hale over to join him, Elise backed away. "You have work to do."

Her intent was to find James and Courtney, and retrieve her purse, but she smacked into a wall of blue shirt and a flak vest.

"Whoa." Shane Wilkins reached out to grab her before she tumbled backward. But his green eyes weren't offering an apology when she looked up. His forehead was creased with concern. "Are you looking for the deputy commissioner?"

Elise's relief was short-lived. Shane would have been smiling if everything was okay. "Have you seen him?"

"He got hurt." He wrapped his fingers around her upper arm and pulled her into the hallway beside him. "I'll take you to him."

Elise glanced over her shoulder to see Denton Hale watching her as Shane, taller and broader than most of the people around him, decided to avoid the open stairs that led up to the lobby and pushed a pathway through the crowd to get to the north emergency stairwell. Once the steel door was safely closed behind them, Elise breathed a sigh of relief.

But she dug in her heels and questioned the change in direction when he turned to the first floor exit instead of continuing up the stairs. "You said we were going upstairs."

Shane pushed open the door to the noise and more natural light of the building's open lobby. Shaking her head, Elise tugged her arm from his grasp and turned toward the stairs. She tipped her head and shouted up the tall stairwell. "George?"

Everything above her seemed rock solid. A good sign, she hoped. But she'd only reached the second step when Shane closed his hands around her waist and lifted her to the floor.

She swatted his hands away. "What are you doing?"

He grabbed her wrist and pulled her toward the exit. "I'll get you out of here."

A spurt of frustrated anger made her strong enough to pull away from his grip. "I thought we were looking for George."

"Stop saying his name like that!" Shane's shout echoed off the concrete walls. "You mean the deputy commissioner?"

Elise retreated when he leaned closer and walked toward her. "Yes. I'll find him myself. You have other duties in the building, I'm sure."

She gasped when her back hit the wall. But he kept coming. "No. I'm saving you."

Elise put up her hands to brace against his chest. "I don't need to be saved."

He was leaning over her now, his handsome face red with anger. "Damn it, yes, you do. You've got a stalker. You've had a Russian mob guy try to kill you."

"Alexsandr didn't threaten me—"

"Shut up!" He slapped his hand across her face and she felt the coppery taste of blood in her mouth.

"Shane?" The übercalm that followed was more frightening than the outburst of anger had been. He squinched up his face and turned away as if he was grappling with impulses that threatened to tear him apart. Elise didn't intend to stay to see which Shane won. She slid along the wall to get away from him. "I'm going to go find Commissioner Madigan," she said in a soft, even tone.

He raked his fingers through his dark blond hair, breathing hard with the effort to control whatever sickness consumed him. She had her hand on the door lever when he turned to her with tears in his eyes. "Do you love him?"

Elise didn't know whether to lie or keep him in reality with her. She opted for reality. "Yes."

Wrong choice.

When she turned to push open the door, he grabbed her from behind and smacked her head against the unbending steel. There was no pain for a split second—all the nerves had been deadened by the blow. But while the ache blossomed and the black door and white walls spun into a sea of gray, Shane snatched her face between his hands and ground his lips over hers in a kiss. "You're mine." He lifted her onto her toes and kissed her again. "I love you."

Elise gripped the door behind her for balance when he dropped her to her feet and backed away. He smiled down at her, as if a beautiful moment had passed between them.

But Elise wiped away his kiss with the back of her hand, taking a smear of blood that had dripped onto her cheek with it. She tenderly touched the gash at her temple, then looked down to see the black gloves that had fallen to the floor. Shane?

She couldn't think of anything to say to properly express her fear and revulsion at the terror and violence he'd put her through. "Why?"

With her vision cleared by anger, she pushed the door lever behind her and swung it open. But before she could call for help or get away, Shane pulled his gun and shoved it into her back. A death grip on her arm yanked her back against his chest and he whispered against her ear, "I'll shoot anyone who tries to help you or keep us apart again."

Then he urged her toward the building's front doors.

"Elise, are you okay?"

She turned at the sound of James Westbrook's voice. With his arm around Courtney Reiter's waist, he was helping her up the main stairs into the lobby.

Even Courtney looked concerned. "That's a bad cut."

A steel barrel jabbed beneath her ribs before she got the chance to say anything. Elise wasn't surprised at how earnest and concerned Shane sounded. "She got hit by some flying debris. I'm taking her to the first aid station."

"I thought they'd set that up downstairs," said James.

Elise looked to the double glass doors. The granite steps out front were completely blocked with the wreckage of a car and an ancient pine tree that had been uprooted from the front lawn.

There were several people between them and the exit Shane had hoped for, some pointing and chatting about the damage, others dealing with the rain coming in through the broken glass.

With a quick breath and glance around him that smelled like desperation, Shane pulled her back toward the stairwell. "There's another aid station upstairs."

James nodded, his eyes narrowed in doubt behind his glasses. "Okay. Call me when you get the chance. Let me know you're okay."

"I need George." Elise mouthed the words as Shane dragged her back to the stairs. It was a plea for her life, and theirs. But she didn't risk saying anything out loud as the stairwell door closed behind them.

GEORGE SHOVED THE mountain of tangled blinds, books and furniture away from the opening beneath the desk, and made a solemn vow to buy himself a sturdy antique like this one for his office upstairs. Assuming he still had an office. And an upstairs.

The rain blowing through the broken window splashed his face and arms as he pushed to his feet and surveyed the damage. There was plenty. But the floor was solid, and the walls of this 1920s steel-and-limestone fortress seemed to still be standing.

But the building damage was the least of his concerns right now. It didn't take him long to decide that what had worked for Shane would work for him. Picking up the metal conference chair the young officer had clocked him with, George swung it against the door, smashing the wood around the lock so he could pull it open, run to the south stairwell and get to Elise.

He'd brushed aside several status reports, and inquiries into the nicks and scratches on his face and hands, and the bruise at his temple, to get downstairs to the storm shelter as quickly as possible. Although there were a few wounded refugees in the men's locker room, most of the area had been cleared out. He certainly wasn't seeing anyone with soft brown waves framing her face and killer legs organizing some kind of team and tackling a list of tasks necessary for a recovery effort.

George propped his hands at his waist and took several deep breaths, keeping his fear at bay. Fine. If he couldn't locate Elise, then he'd look for Shane.

He stopped the first uniformed officer who walked past. Denton Hale wasn't much of a go-getter on his own time, but he snapped to when George called his name. "Which one is Wilkins's locker?"

Hale led him to the end of the row. "This one, sir."

"Can we cut that lock?"

Hale called over a maintenance man with a toolbox and cut off the lock with a set of bolt cutters.

When George pulled open the metal door, he swore one choice, biting word.

Hanging from a hook at the back of the locker was a dried-up yellow rose. In the gym bag at the bottom he found a pair of lacy blue panties and a ton of pictures. All of them of Elise—waving to the camera across a parking lot, walking her dog, lounging on the deck in her backyard, eating a salad in Pitsaeli's Restaurant, standing on her front porch, hugging Spike, looking wary and afraid.

A box on the top shelf held something even more disturbing—stacks of love poems and letters, all saying variations of the same thing.

I love you.

You're mine.

We belong together.

No one will keep us apart.

When the bile in his throat receded and he

could speak again, George turned to Officer Hale. "When was the last time you saw Elise?"

"About fifteen minutes ago." He nodded toward the locker room exit. "She went looking for you. Wilkins was with her."

"Shane Wilkins?"

"Yeah."

"Do you know which way they went?"

"Your last known location was upstairs. I'm sure they went that way. They headed to the north end of the building. She was worried sick about you." Hale pointed to the drops of blood on George's damp shirt. "Sir, you're hurt."

"Just a few cuts and a bump on the head. Give me your building keys." When George gestured for him to hurry and hand them over, Denton unhooked the ring of keys and dropped them into his palm. "Are you carrying a spare gun?"

"Yeah." Hale nodded and pulled a Smith & Wesson from the ankle holster beneath his pant leg.

George held it down and away and checked the loaded magazine and weight of the weapon before sliding it into his own holster. "Get on the horn and find out if my nephew, Detective Fensom, is in the building. Tell him and any of his friends to meet me upstairs. I may need backup."

"Sir?"

George strode into the hallway, with Hale hurrying along beside him. "You want to guarantee your job, and get those lousy performance evaluations off your record?"

"Yes, sir."

"Make that call, then get your butt upstairs and help me find Elise."

ELISE COULD SENSE Shane's growing agitation with every step. When his getaway out the front door, parking garage or fire escape exits had been thwarted by crowds of people or storm damage that would require him to holster his gun and risk Elise screaming for help or making a break for it, Shane had decided to head up the stairs.

But every floor they tried to enter had cops on it, searching through rooms. Elise recognized some of the detectives and uniformed officers. A. J. Rodriguez and Josh Taylor, detectives who'd worked together for years, were on the third floor, righting desks and chairs and cubicle walls. Shane avoided a tall K-9 officer and his German shepherd peeking into a room on the sixth floor. She saw Nick Fensom's stocky figure. He was wrestling with his cell phone to get some decent reception on the eighth floor leading to George's office. But she didn't dare call out to him. The hand crushing her arm and the gun bruising her ribs wouldn't allow her to risk it.

Her lungs were beginning to ache with their steady climb. But, like a cornered animal, Shane seemed to think he had no place to go but up. When he heard voices on the stairs two flights beneath them, he forced her into double time, taking her up the last few stairs onto the roof.

When he pushed open the last door, Elise instinctively drew back from the slap of rain on her face. It was pouring outside. The air smelled of dust and ozone, but felt cleaner than the stale musk of Shane's nervous perspiration. Streaks of lightning forked across the sky, pricking the hairs on her forearms and at the back of her neck. Thunder rumbled loudly, as if a marching band was waiting on the roof to greet them.

Shane released her just once, to push aside the wreckage of a satellite dish that littered the steps leading up to the helicopter pad, air conditioners and power units that served the entire building. She'd only backed a few feet away before his gun was trained on her again. He reached down his hand to her, leaving her no choice but to join him up top.

The rain soaked her to the skin in seconds and the wind whipping through her hair made her shiver. "What are we doing up here, Shane? There's no place left to go."

"We're together." He had her by the arm again, adding five more bruises to the marks he'd already left there. "That's all that matters to me."

He ducked his head against the driving rain and hiked across the empty helipad to the concrete wall at the edge of the building. "Shane, what are you doing? There's lightning up here. I don't think it's safe."

Elise tried to pull away when he leaned over the side. "Look at our city," he said, the tone of his voice matching the drama of the sky above them. "I thought it'd be in shambles. But it's still standing. Cars are moving, see?" He pulled her to the wall, and for the first time that day, she prayed he had an unbreakable hold on her. "See?"

Elise forced herself to look. She saw broken windows and toppled trees, lines of streets with streetlights on and others that were dark—and way too much distance between her and the ground below. Magnificent view. If she wanted to die.

"Shane, you're scaring me."

"What? Why?" He let her back away from the edge, but sat down on top of the wall, pulling her onto the slick seat beside him. *Don't look behind you. Don't look down.* Shane moved his hand to her knee, where his grip proved just as effective at holding her captive as her arm had been. "I love you. And you love me. I won't let you get hurt. I'll save you."

The rain loosened the blood that had dried on her temple and cheek, and it dripped into her lap. So this was how her sorry, second-guessing life would end. "How do you know I love you?"

The wind buffeted them and the rain chilled. Shane rested the gun in his lap, with the barrel pointed at her. And he smiled. "Every day, you talk to me. Every day, you smile. I'm one in a million, you said."

She said hi to him every morning because he was the first person she'd see when she stepped off the eighth-floor elevator. She talked to him because they worked together. She smiled because…she smiled at nearly every person she met. It had become a brave mask to hide behind when she felt unsure of herself or needed a boost of self-confidence.

"We've always been friends—"

"It's more than that. Your loyalty is one of the things I treasure most about you. I've had other people say they love me. But they didn't. They lied to me. They left.

"I've got my degree," he went on. "Soon I'll have my master's. I'll make detective and I'll be commissioner one day. And you'll be right there with me. Supporting me, just like you always have."

When he took her hand and got down on one knee, Elise nearly retched. "Shane, don't."

When tears joined the rain rolling down her cheeks, he smiled. "I love you, Elise Brown."

"Put the gun down, son. Step away from the edge of the roof."

"George!" Her relief was so intense that she nearly forgot her precarious perch. But the stony eyes boring into hers across the roof sent a warning instead of a promise.

In a flash of movement, like Jekyll and Hyde, Shane jumped to his feet and pulled Elise in front of him like a shield. Although he stood a head taller, she imagined the target he presented to the gun George aimed at him wasn't very big.

"Get back!" Shane warned, pushing his gun against her neck. "I don't want you here."

Whether he was yelling at George or the other detectives and uniformed officers she saw climbing up the stairs and taking positions beside him, she couldn't tell.

George's rock steady hands never wavered. "Elise, are you hurt?"

She sniffed back her tears as she clawed at the arm cinched around her throat. *Be brave.* This was her last chance to seize the life she wanted with no regrets or second-guessing. "Nothing serious. Yet."

"I wouldn't hurt her," Shane insisted, despite the blood and bruises and terror. "I love her."

George took two steps across the roof. "Shane, this isn't going to end well if you don't put down that gun and let her go."

How could she help? How could she make George's job easier? How could she save herself?

And then she knew. "It's all right, George. Shane and I have been talking. We're friends." She erased the tremor from her voice, blinked the rain from her eyes so she could see that face filled with so much life experience and love. "We're more than friends. He's been watching over me. I think he wants to marry me."

Shane's arm eased its choke hold on her neck. "What? What are you saying?"

"Weren't you about to propose to me?"

George was slowly shaking his head. "Elise, what are you doing?" He put out his hand to warn the other officers to keep their distance, then cradled the gun again. "Honey?"

"If this is a trick..." Shane tapped her neck

with the barrel of his gun, reminding her of his control over her.

"I will never leave you." Elise petted the arm she'd dug her nails into just moments earlier. "You promised me a lot, Shane. But you have to ask. A girl likes to be asked."

She felt him nod behind her. And then, with a streak of lightning cutting through the sky over their heads, he took her hand and knelt down. But when she stepped to the side, he knew.

She'd lied.

Shane clamped his hand over her wrist, swinging the gun toward George, and charging toward the edge of the roof, dragging her behind him. "She's mine!"

"Drop it, Shane!"

Before her knees hit the wall, gunfire rang out, drowning out the thunder.

Elise couldn't count how many bullets there were. But she felt the spatter of blood on her neck, and the tug on her arm as Shane's body crumpled to the roof and pulled her down with him.

"Elise!" George was at her side in an instant. He kicked Shane's gun from his lifeless hand before holstering his own. "What a damn waste."

Before she could get to her feet, he scooped

her up into his arms and carried her away from her captor while other officers swarmed in to secure the scene.

"Put me down, George." She pushed against his chest. "Put me down."

"What's wrong? I'm trying to get you out of the rain." When she pushed again, he stopped and set her down beside the broken satellite dish at the top of the stairs. "Are you hurt?" He clasped her face, checked the cut on her head, ran his fingers along her arms, cursing at the bruises already forming there. "What did he do to you?"

Elise threw her arms around his neck and hugged him so tightly, even the rain couldn't fall between them. "This is what I need. I need you to hold me."

"Okay, honey." He sighed in relief, folding his arms around her at last. He pulled her into his chest, surrounded her with his body and rubbed his smooth cheek against hers. "Okay. I've got you. I need to hold you, too."

They stood together like that for endless moments, cheek to cheek and heart to heart. Elise cried out her stress and fear, and absorbed George's strength. When she was spent, when she was breathing normally against him, he leaned back, his face as grave as she'd ever seen it. And then he was kissing her, hard, thoroughly. Just as quickly, he tore his mouth from hers to press a far gentler kiss beside the wound on her forehead. "Damn it, woman, I won't survive another day like this."

Elise curled her fingers into his collar, squeezing the water from it and smoothing it against his neck and chest. "Dealing with a psychopath?"

"No."

She glanced up, surprised by his answer. "Surviving a tornado?"

"Thinking I was going to lose you."

This time, Elise stretched onto her toes and kissed him, sliding her fingers into his hair and pledging with every stroke on his lips, every slide of her tongue that she was no one's but his. Elise felt the rain running against her scalp beneath her hair. She heard the thunder rumbling overhead. But all she knew was the taste and power of this man's kiss.

"Damn, Uncle George—get a room." Nick Fensom walked up beside them and squeezed his uncle's shoulder. It was a gesture of love and relief, and probably the only way he could interrupt this relationship that wasn't supposed to exist. "Does she need a medic?"

George never took his eyes off her. "Do you?"

Elise shook her head. "Not yet. I probably need stitches, but I'm not ready to go down yet." She never took her eyes off George, either. "We need to discuss *this* first."

While a smile spread across George's handsome face for her, his voice commanded Nick and the others. "Clear the roof. Get him off my building. Find the next senior officer on-site and tell him to get me a status report on casualties and damage." At the last second, he turned to Nick. "In twenty minutes."

Nick grinned. "I can buy you twenty minutes, old man."

Someone brought a morgue bag and others carried the troubled officer's body down the stairs. A few detectives snapped pictures of the scene, but it was raining too hard for them to preserve any evidence beyond the body itself. Elise tucked her head beneath George's chin and held on until they were all alone.

But it was George who spoke first.

"Twenty minutes may not be enough time to say everything I want to." In the pouring rain, with a streak of lightning dancing over the skyline that still stood tall and proud over Kansas City, George Madigan spoke the words in his heart. "For years I've been trying to turn myself into someone I'm not. Because that's what

Court wanted. But you get me. I can be the man I want to be with you—the man I'm meant to be. You needed me to be that man. I'm a cop. Always have been, always will be. Okay, so I'm a cop who puts together budget sheets and personnel charts, but I'm still a cop."

"Protect and serve your city. That's you, George. I never doubted it for a moment."

With a wry laugh, he smoothed the wet hair off her face and tucked it behind her ear. "Not even when I did. You and I fit together in a way no other woman has. You make me happy. And whole again. I need you, Elise Brown."

She spoke the words in her heart, too. "I need you."

And somehow, with the way he was kissing her, with the way she couldn't let go of him, "I need you" became "I love you."

He left her mouth to lap up the cool rain from along her jaw and warm the skin there. "I know you've got a thing about dating your boss—"

"There are KCPD rules and regulations to consider." She nibbled on his chin, kissed the grooves of laughter beside his eyes. "You're a superior officer. You have to uphold them."

"I'm going to marry you even if I have to fire you. Understood?"

Elise blinked the rain from her lashes and framed his face, too, smiling up at him. "You could just transfer me to another office."

"I'm in charge of that stuff, aren't I. I could do that."

"Yes, you could."

"It might mean a cut in pay. For now. Or getting stuck with some tyrant for a boss. But I will fire his ass if he gets out of line—"

Elise pressed a finger against his lips to hush him. "Do you think money is what I want? Do you think I can't handle some grumpy old curmudgeon? Do you think there's an office out there I can't run?"

"I'm going to miss you at work, Elise." His smile faded for a moment, and the man who never minced words seemed unsure of what to say. "But I'll see you in bed every night and across the breakfast table every morning. Right?"

"Is that an official proposal, Deputy Commissioner?"

"Yes. If you'll have an old man."

"I won't." Elise stretched up on tiptoe to kiss his lips into a smile. "But I'll have you."

* * * * *

LARGER-PRINT BOOKS!

GET 2 FREE LARGER-PRINT NOVELS PLUS
2 FREE GIFTS!

HARLEQUIN®

Romance

From the Heart, For the Heart

YES! Please send me 2 FREE LARGER-PRINT Harlequin® Romance novels and my 2 FREE gifts (gifts are worth about $10). After receiving them, if I don't wish to receive any more books, I can return the shipping statement marked "cancel." If I don't cancel, I will receive 4 brand-new novels every month and be billed just $4.84 per book in the U.S. or $5.24 per book in Canada. That's a savings of at least 19% off the cover price! It's quite a bargain! Shipping and handling is just 50¢ per book in the U.S. and 75¢ per book in Canada.* I understand that accepting the 2 free books and gifts places me under no obligation to buy anything. I can always return a shipment and cancel at any time. Even if I never buy another book, the two free books and gifts are mine to keep forever.

119/319 HDN F43Y

Name _____ (PLEASE PRINT)

Address _____ Apt. #

City _____ State/Prov. _____ Zip/Postal Code

Signature (if under 18, a parent or guardian must sign)

Mail to the **Harlequin® Reader Service:**
IN U.S.A.: P.O. Box 1867, Buffalo, NY 14240-1867
IN CANADA: P.O. Box 609, Fort Erie, Ontario L2A 5X3
Want to try two free books from another line?
Call 1-800-873-8635 or visit www.ReaderService.com.

* Terms and prices subject to change without notice. Prices do not include applicable taxes. Sales tax applicable in N.Y. Canadian residents will be charged applicable taxes. Offer not valid in Quebec. This offer is limited to one order per household. Not valid for current subscribers to Harlequin Romance Larger-Print books. All orders subject to credit approval. Credit or debit balances in a customer's account(s) may be offset by any other outstanding balance owed by or to the customer. Please allow 4 to 6 weeks for delivery. Offer available while quantities last.

Your Privacy—The Harlequin® Reader Service is committed to protecting your privacy. Our Privacy Policy is available online at www.ReaderService.com or upon request from the Harlequin Reader Service.

We make a portion of our mailing list available to reputable third parties that offer products we believe may interest you. If you prefer that we not exchange your name with third parties, or if you wish to clarify or modify your communication preferences, please visit us at www.ReaderService.com/consumerschoice or write to us at Harlequin Reader Service Preference Service, P.O. Box 9062, Buffalo, NY 14269. Include your complete name and address.

HRLP13R

LARGER-PRINT BOOKS!

**GET 2 FREE
LARGER-PRINT NOVELS
PLUS 2 FREE
MYSTERY GIFTS**

Love Inspired
SUSPENSE
RIVETING INSPIRATIONAL ROMANCE

Larger-print novels are now available...

YES! Please send me 2 FREE LARGER-PRINT Love Inspired® Suspense novels and my 2 FREE mystery gifts (gifts are worth about $10). After receiving them, if I don't wish to receive any more books, I can return the shipping statement marked "cancel." If I don't cancel, I will receive 4 brand-new novels every month and be billed just $5.24 per book in the U.S. or $5.74 per book in Canada. That's a savings of at least 23% off the cover price. It's quite a bargain! Shipping and handling is just 50¢ per book in the U.S. and 75¢ per book in Canada.* I understand that accepting the 2 free books and gifts places me under no obligation to buy anything. I can always return a shipment and cancel at any time. Even if I never buy another book, the two free books and gifts are mine to keep forever.

110/310 IDN F5CC

Name	(PLEASE PRINT)	
Address		Apt. #
City	State/Prov.	Zip/Postal Code

Signature (if under 18, a parent or guardian must sign)

Mail to the **Harlequin® Reader Service:**
IN U.S.A.: P.O. Box 1867, Buffalo, NY 14240-1867
IN CANADA: P.O. Box 609, Fort Erie, Ontario L2A 5X3

**Are you a current subscriber to Love Inspired Suspense books
and want to receive the larger-print edition?
Call 1-800-873-8635 or visit www.ReaderService.com.**

* Terms and prices subject to change without notice. Prices do not include applicable taxes. Sales tax applicable in N.Y. Canadian residents will be charged applicable taxes. Offer not valid in Quebec. This offer is limited to one order per household. Not valid for current subscribers to Love Inspired Suspense larger-print books. All orders subject to credit approval. Credit or debit balances in a customer's account(s) may be offset by any other outstanding balance owed by or to the customer. Please allow 4 to 6 weeks for delivery. Offer available while quantities last.

Your Privacy—The Harlequin® Reader Service is committed to protecting your privacy. Our Privacy Policy is available online at www.ReaderService.com or upon request from the Harlequin Reader Service.

We make a portion of our mailing list available to reputable third parties that offer products we believe may interest you. If you prefer that we not exchange your name with third parties, or if you wish to clarify or modify your communication preferences, please visit us at www.ReaderService.com/consumerchoice or write to us at Harlequin Reader Service Preference Service, P.O. Box 9062, Buffalo, NY 14269. Include your complete name and address.

LISLPDIR13R

ReaderService.com

Manage your account online!

- Review your order history
- Manage your payments
- Update your address

*We've designed
the Harlequin® Reader Service
website just for you.*

Enjoy all the features!

- Reader excerpts from any series
- Respond to mailings and special monthly offers
- Discover new series available to you
- Browse the Bonus Bucks catalog
- Share your feedback

Visit us at:

ReaderService.com